"Hang on!"

Brooke wanted to scream and would have if she hadn't feared startling Colt and causing him to make an error. She could see the delivery truck pretty clearly in her side mirror when their SUV turned to the right. Then the larger truck clipped the rear bumper of Colt's SUV.

It shimmied. He corrected and kept it on the road.

Managing to turn in her seat enough to look out the rear window, past the specially constructed compartment designed to keep Sampson safe, she caught a glimpse of something that stole her breath.

"What is it? What did you see?"

"That driver."

"What about him?"

"Not him. *Her.* It's a woman—a̶n̶d̶ ̶s̶h̶e̶ ̶l̶o̶o̶k̶s̶ ̶l̶i̶ke me."

Valerie Hansen was thirty when she awoke to the presence of the Lord in her life and turned to Jesus. She now lives in a renovated farmhouse on the breathtakingly beautiful Ozark Plateau of Arkansas and is privileged to share her personal faith by telling the stories of her heart for Love Inspired. Life doesn't get much better than that!

Books by Valerie Hansen

Love Inspired Suspense

Pacific Northwest K-9 Unit

Scent of Truth

Emergency Responders

Fatal Threat
Marked for Revenge
On the Run
Christmas Vendetta
Serial Threat

Rocky Mountain K-9 Unit

Ready to Protect

True Blue K-9 Unit: Brooklyn

Tracking a Kidnapper

True Blue K-9 Unit

Trail of Danger

Visit the Author Profile page at LoveInspired.com for more titles.

SCENT OF TRUTH

VALERIE HANSEN

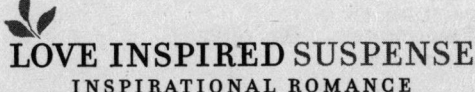

LOVE INSPIRED SUSPENSE
INSPIRATIONAL ROMANCE

Special thanks and acknowledgment are given to Valerie Hansen for her contribution to the Pacific Northwest K-9 Unit miniseries.

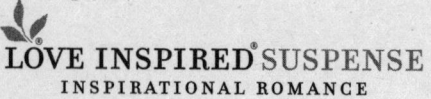

LOVE INSPIRED® SUSPENSE

INSPIRATIONAL ROMANCE

Recycling programs for this product may not exist in your area.

ISBN-13: 978-1-335-58768-8

Scent of Truth

Love Inspired
22 Adelaide St. West, 41st Floor
Toronto, Ontario M5H 4E3, Canada
www.LoveInspired.com

Printed in U.S.A.

I am made all things to all men,
that I might by all means save some.
—1 Corinthians 9:22

To Joe, who took me to every state in North America and introduced me to the grandeur of the National Parks. And to the men and women who guard their beauty.

ONE

Shadows lengthened, shrouding the well-traveled paths through the old-growth forest and accentuating the lingering chill of a late spring. Mount Rainier National Park Ranger Brooke Stevens took a breath of the icy air, shivered and turned up the collar of her forest-green jacket.

Portions of the branching trails she was inspecting glistened with moonlit ice. Nature hikes and interactions with park visitors kept her busy during the day, but at night—at night details of the recent double murder came flooding back. Truth to tell, no one was safe in spite of the recurring presence of officers from a K-9 unit that covered three Washington State national parks, hers included.

Stamping snow off her boots, Brooke bent to pick up a discarded candy wrapper and an empty chip bag. The paper crinkled as she stuffed it into her plastic trash bag. A twig snapped somewhere close by. Brooke froze. The added weight of ice on fragile limbs could make them crack like that, of course, but the sun had melted most of the treetop accumulations.

Tendrils of fear crept up her neck like the uncurling fiddleheads of nearby ferns. Fellow rangers who knew she was out here wouldn't be concerned unless she used her radio to call for backup. If she gave in to jumpy nerves and admitted being afraid when there was nobody actually stalking her, she'd never live it down.

Listening, she held her breath. Her pulse thudded. The nearby woods were so silent it was creepy. Nothing moved. No birds called, no squirrels scampered—not even the hoot of an owl or screechy yip of a fox broke the heavy silence. There was only her, a lone, unarmed ranger.

If she turned back now she'd be shirking her duty to keep the trails clean. Still, what might she face if she went ahead and completed her rounds? Which was better, carrying on in spite of an eerie feeling or looking like a fool by reporting danger when she had no proof?

She started to reach for the radio clipped to her belt. Something crashed into her from behind. One gloved hand held her arm while another tightened at her throat. She tried to twist away and loudly screamed, "No-o-o-o!"

A faint reply echoed, then another.

"Help!" she screamed.

Brooke's dark-clad assailant shoved her aside and bolted, then slipped on the slick trail and clambered off on all fours like a clumsy bear cub.

Dizzy, she braced to defend herself. Instead of the ski-masked man who had tried to grab her, however, a pair of concerned-looking hikers jogged into view, coming from the direction of Longmire bridge.

"Are you all right?" The first young man dropped his day pack and approached.

"I am now," Brooke said. "It's not safe out here after dark. Come on. I'll escort you guys down."

"Did you hear a scream?" the second hiker asked.

"That was me." Brooke paused to catch her breath a bit more.

"What happened?"

"I'll fill you in as we walk. Let's get out of here, all of us, before we freeze."

After leading her small party back to the partially open campground near the ranger station while answering their questions as best she could, Brooke saw them safely settled, then reported the incident to her superior, the head ranger, Georgia Henning, via radio.

"All right," the older woman said, sounding less than pleased to be disturbed after office hours. "Go back to your cabin and warm up. I'll send someone over to take your statement while it's fresh in your mind."

"I doubt I'll forget," Brooke replied, trying to quell any hint of sarcasm.

Henning's comeback was devoid of the humor that might have made it easier to take. "Some people adapt to the wilderness well and some don't, Stevens. You can't lead groups of hikers on effective nature walks if you're jumping at shadows."

"Yeah, well, this shadow grabbed me. I didn't imagine it." Brooke had continued to walk swiftly as they talked and was almost home.

"If you insist. You have witnesses?"

"There were a couple of hikers out there who heard me scream and rushed over, but the guy who grabbed me fled the scene before they arrived. I'm the only one who saw what he did." Closer to her cabin, she noted clusters of footprints in the snow and mud, particularly at the base of a window. "Whoa. Hold on."

"What? Stevens, report."

"I was blaming my feelings of being watched on the memory of that couple who were murdered in the park last month. It looks like my jitters were for a good reason. Somebody left tracks all around my cabin."

"Explain."

"You almost have to see this for yourself. There are so many prints here it looks like somebody held a family reunion."

"Any chance we can follow them?"

Brooke swept her light over the uneven ground and shined it into the thicket at the base of some smaller red cedar and western hemlock trees. "Maybe. I can see boot prints leading away."

"All right. The cabin is secure?"

"Looks like it. If I go up on the porch I may destroy evidence."

"Okay. I already have rangers responding. I'll be out as soon as I've contacted our park K-9 unit and ordered a tracking dog. In the meantime, stay out in the open, where you can see and be seen. Help will be there in moments."

"Affirmative." Brooke was glad her boss was so organized even if that trait did drive the Mt. Rainier ranger staff up the wall. At this point, her only regret was leaving the site of her attack on the trail instead of calling it in from there and waiting for official assistance.

She drew a shaky breath. A young couple, Stacey Stark and Jonas Digby, had been shot a mere forty or fifty yards from where she had been jumped tonight, and their killer was still at large. At this point in the ongoing investigation, every clue must be carefully examined and she had blown it when she'd left the scene of her assault.

Sounds of approaching vehicles echoed in the distance. Brooke had to admit she didn't care who was coming, even if the responders included her by-the-book boss, because there would soon be one of the magnificent working dogs, too. Picturing the impressive German shepherd she'd seen at the Stark Lodge and hoping he was the K-9 they sent, she folded her arms across her chest for warmth and shivered. This promised to be a long, long night.

* * *

K-9 Officer Colt Maxwell and his bloodhound, Sampson, had been temporarily placed at the Stark Lodge near Mount Rainier National Park as part of the investigation into a double murder the previous month. Usually he was paired up with his colleague Danica Hayes and her protection dog, Hutch, but since they were out on a different assignment that evening, Colt was assigned to respond to the call inside the park with fellow officer Willow Bates and her K-9, Star, a German shorthair pointer.

"I'll go talk to the ranger," Colt told Willow as he pulled his PNK9 SUV to a stop behind one of the official park vehicles. "No sense both of us and our dogs getting chilled if they don't need Star's skills."

"Call if we can help," Willow said.

He nodded, and then circled behind the SUV. He released Sampson from the specially constructed safety area in the rear and snapped on a tracking lead. All floppy ears and drool, the bloodhound jumped down with a plop and looked up at Colt, clearly eager to work. There was always an underlying sense of excitement whenever he and his K-9 were called to the scene of a crime even though Sampson was rarely asked to track a live human being. Most of his work involved finding the deceased, and he was very good at locating bodies.

Several rangers stood guard at access points to a small cabin. Headlights and spotlights from park vehicles shone on the yard, casting shadows in the unevenly packed snow. Colt kept Sampson at heel as he sought out the person in charge to report for duty.

The head ranger, Georgia Henning, was facing a younger female ranger when Colt approached. Nobody had to be close by to hear their conversation because it was rather heated, particularly on Henning's part.

Toe-to-toe with her staff member, she pointed. "Are you sure these footprints weren't here when you left?"

Although the younger woman spoke softly, her voice was firm. "Positive. This mess would be hard to overlook."

"Hmm. I suppose they could have been caused by wandering park visitors. Some of them are quite nosy."

As Henning went on speaking, she raised her voice and directed her attention to Colt and the rangers. "All right. I want a cordon around this whole scene, particularly where you can see disturbances. When in doubt, take in a wider area. Then everybody stand back and hold your positions. Now that the K-9 is here we'll let him lead off."

Colt could feel the energy from his partner traveling up the leash and see how eager he was to get going. He stepped forward. The younger ranger was trembling so he paused to ask for background. "Is this your cabin?"

"Yes."

The name tag on her uniform said *Stevens*, which was enough to trigger a memory of having met her before, not that he hadn't recognized her by sight the moment he'd arrived. Even all bundled up against the cold he could see locks of her auburn hair peeking out. Both that and her freckles were a dead giveaway.

He offered his hand. "Colt Maxwell. And this is Sampson."

"I'm Brooke. Brooke Stevens. I think we've met before."

"We have. I was here for the Stark-Digby homicides."

Henning raised an eyebrow at the bloodhound as if just now recognizing him. "Hold on. I told your chief we needed a tracking dog."

"Affirmative. Sampson can do that, too, as long as he has a scent to follow."

"If you say so."

He smiled slightly, aware of how most people doubted

the extraordinary feats their unit's K-9s were capable of until they'd seen success after success. "Was the cabin broken into?"

Brooke answered. "I don't think so. It's this trampling all over the yard that worried me after…"

"After?" Seeing her look to her superior for affirmation, he wondered what they were *not* saying.

"There was an incident on one of the trails tonight," Brooke finally told him. "Someone grabbed me. I should have stayed there and radioed for backup, I know, but two hikers had come along and the guy ran off. All I could think about was getting home." Gesturing with her whole arm, she added, "And now this."

Sampson was sniffing the air, impatient, but Colt wasn't quite ready to put him to work. "Do you think the two events could be connected? That the guy who grabbed you was lurking around your cabin and then followed you?"

"I don't know," the pretty ranger said with a shrug, pressing the edges of her jacket collar closer to her ears.

"All right. We'll start next to the cabin. Have you been up on the porch recently?"

"I got close. I never thought…"

"It's okay. Sampson can sort out scents the way some people make a beeline for the cinnamon roll store in a mall." To his relief, that comment caused Brooke to give him a fleeting smile, even if her boss did look a bit put out. Well, too bad. Mild humor was his go-to response to put people at ease in almost any situation. It had worked well in the past and he was thankful that his personality allowed some levity despite warranted seriousness. Everyone benefitted from it.

Georgia Henning spoke up. "I've kept my people away from tracks leading into the forest. If you start there you may find a cleaner trail."

"Good. Show me."

She pointed. "There. And over there."

"Those aren't normal access points?"

Brooke was shaking her head. "No. I always come in from the campground by way of the road, even when I'm walking. It's easier, and that way I don't damage the meadows."

"Okay." Colt gave her another smile, hoping to reassure her, then commanded Sampson to heel and started off, intending to skirt the perimeter.

He was halfway to the set of tracks he could see as uneven depressions in a drift of snow beneath one of the Douglas fir trees when his K-9 began trying to pull him to the side.

Colt paused to study the dog. He knew his partner as well as he knew himself and there was clearly something on Sampson's mind besides footprints. Nevertheless, he kept the dog close to maintain full control until he was ready to listen.

Sampson glanced up at him with those big, brown, limpid eyes and whined. If he could have talked, Colt figured he'd be calling his handler names.

"All right, boy. You're the boss."

"No!" Henning called after him, "Not that way."

Fixated on his K-9, Colt ignored her. Sampson was basically making straight for the woodpile behind the cabin. Park residents heated primarily by burning wood rather than having propane delivered or pay for electricity, particularly in the simple dwellings assigned to staff. Consequently, there were stacks of cut and split firewood all over the compound and more for sale to campers at the in-park concessions. Otherwise, visitors would decimate the natural vegetation looking for something to burn.

Nose to the ground, Sampson rounded the end of the

stacked wood, sniffed a particularly large mound of snow, sat down and whined.

Colt rewarded him with his favorite little stuffed toy, a worn pink bunny. Then he motioned to the closest ranger and called out, "You'd better get your boss over here and tell her to notify CSI."

The younger man stood gaping at the mound. Colt looked back at the resident of the cabin and locked eyes with Brooke Stevens. Her lips were parted, too, as if she knew exactly what the K-9 had found. He couldn't wrap his mind around the possibility that such a naturally lovely woman could be a criminal, but this development wasn't looking good for her.

Sampson was never wrong. Colt had no doubt the snow was covering a body. The very dead kind.

TWO

Brooke's mind was whirling, her mouth was dry and she was trembling all the way to her core. Bypassing the taped line around her cabin despite orders to stay back, she joined the K-9 cop and his dog. Frozen ground didn't allow for grave digging, but snow could be moved fairly easily if a body needed to be covered, which is what apparently had occurred here. At her home. Perhaps even while she slept.

Shovels were removing more and more dirty snow and mud. A black plastic trash bag split open and a camouflage-patterned jacket sleeve was revealed, then a hand, which was gray, stiff and wrinkled. Bile rose in her throat. She wanted to turn away, to avoid seeing more, yet she couldn't make herself do it.

This was the stuff of night terrors, of horrible, warped imaginings that were far worse than reality. Only this time, the images were real. There was a body hidden in her yard and she had no idea why, or where it had come from.

She stifled the urge to shout her innocence at the top of her lungs. Doing that, of course, was ridiculous. Anybody who knew her, really knew her, would know she wasn't capable of hurting people. She didn't even *argue* with anyone if she could avoid it.

Thoughts of arguments brought visions of her parents' negative reactions to her decision to quit business school and become a park ranger. She wasn't designed to sit behind a big desk and be a cutthroat oil executive like her father. It was too bad she hadn't been able to make him see that when she'd changed career paths.

Childhood feelings and memories caused Brooke to suddenly yearn to phone her mother. She resisted. True innocence would clear her. That was how the law worked, right?

She considered the bloodhound, who was now acting like a happy puppy, bouncing around on the end of a long lead and shaking the soggy stuffed animal toy. Seeing his innocent exuberance made it easier to find her voice. "I'm Brooke Stevens."

"So you said."

"I did, didn't I? Guess I'm a little addled tonight."

"That's understandable," the K-9 officer said with a subtle bow.

"Your dog is beautiful. Can I touch him?"

"Not while he's in uniform," Colt warned. "He's a working K-9 when he's wearing his vest and harness, and he knows it."

She stuffed her hands back into her pockets. "Sorry."

"No problem."

"Good to see you again," Brooke said, before rethinking her response. "This is not the best of circumstances, but you know what I mean."

"I do."

For the first time since his arrival, Colt seemed to soften a little but quickly sobered, gesturing at the snow pile. "Do you know who that might be?"

"Not a clue. Sorry."

"For your sake I hope that's still true once we get a look at a face," he said. "Most murders involve individuals who are acquainted, family or friends."

"That's so sad."

When he said, "Yes, it is," she could tell how deeply he meant it. He went on as if suddenly remembering the words in a scripted interrogation. "I take it you have no coworkers missing."

She shook her head. "Not that I know of. Superintendent Henning is the one to ask about staff. She keeps close tabs on everything and everybody."

Colt quirked a smile, averting his face so only Brooke could see. "No doubt. She strikes me as the kind of person who'd put a dish of candy on her desk then give you a dirty look if you took a piece."

Brooke nodded. "I've never thought of it quite that way but you're right. I suppose being persnickety is a desired leadership trait."

"Now there's a word I haven't heard in a long time. Where are you from, Stevens?"

"It's a long story. What about you?"

"Headquarters for our unit is Olympia."

She knew he was aware she'd been asking a personal question and had chosen to pretend otherwise. Well, fine. She wasn't any more eager to discuss roots than he apparently was, although she did wonder about his background. There was something appealing about the intensity in his deep blue eyes, as if they masked a secret that only he was privy to.

And speaking of secrets… Brooke's gaze darted back to the activity taking place. Thoughts of another innocent person losing his or her life, especially amid the grandeur of this national park, hurt her heart. Unshed tears gathered.

"It'll be okay," Colt offered, stepping slightly closer and lightly touching the sleeve of her coat. "Don't worry."

When she looked up at him, telltale drops of sadness escaped to trickle down her cheeks. She sniffled and whisked them away.

"I hope so. This whole thing is unbelievable."

"Whole thing?"

"The crime wave. We haven't solved the double homicide in the park last month, let alone found the reasons behind other recent suspicious activity. I mean, a certain number of daredevil types get hurt every year when they pit themselves against the mountain or underestimate our lakes and rivers and drown, but this year is different. The problem this year isn't due to only foolish bravado—it's apparently being caused by an enemy of law and order, as well. There's a big difference."

"Do you think all the cases you mentioned are connected?"

Brooke shrugged. "I don't see how they can be. I mean, what can they possibly have in common?" She broke off, staring blankly at the digging activity.

The expression on the K-9 cop's face was telling. He asked, "How can you know they don't when we don't have an ID on whoever's buried here?"

"I can't." Realizing how guilty her casual comment made her look, she blushed. "I just meant…"

Colt stopped her with a raised hand. "Don't say anything else before you consult an attorney."

"What?" She was incensed. "I don't need a lawyer. I haven't done anything wrong."

Although he said, "Good," his expression showed doubt.

Brooke just stood there, her mouth gaping. A feeling of being watched caused her to scan the people nearby and those waiting by the road. Every eye was on her as if they were waiting for her to blurt out a confession.

Flinging both arms wide, she screeched then shouted, "I am *not* guilty!"

* * *

The outburst from the usually personable ranger surprised Colt and he wasn't the only one. Sampson stopped playing and returned to his side, awaiting instructions. Everybody close enough to hear stopped moving, stopped working.

Georgia Henning trotted up and took Brooke by the arm. "Enough. You'll wait in my car while we finish."

Noting the set of Brooke's jaw and the way she'd planted her feet, Colt decided to interfere before the situation escalated. "I've got this," he said. "I'd really like her to be here to see if she recognizes the victim's face when it's uncovered, if you don't mind."

Hesitancy on the part of the older ranger didn't surprise him. After all, her position did essentially outrank his, even though they were members of different law-enforcement agencies. Colt patted the closed holster at his waist in unspoken assurance. "I'll take responsibility."

In the few seconds it took Georgia to make up her mind to relinquish control, Colt tried to comfort Brooke with a reassuring look. It fell flat. By the time her boss turned on her heel and stalked away, Brooke was clearly boiling mad.

"Save some of that anger to help melt the snow," Colt said.

"What?"

He chuckled. "Lady, if you could redirect the flaming arrows of injured pride shooting from your eyes, the whole park would be ready for wildflowers months early."

"It's not pride, it's truth. I know I'm innocent."

"Then take a deep breath, settle down and wait with me while the crime-scene people finish their job. Stats show that guilty folks are quicker to fly off the handle than the ones with nothing to hide."

He could tell by the color infusing her cheeks that she

was about to counter his statistics. Well, fine. Anything that kept her from implicating herself was okay with him, even if it meant he was about to get a talking-to. He'd spent his early childhood being berated and blamed for things he hadn't done. He was a pro at listening to punishing accusations without taking them to heart.

Colt closed his eyes for a nanosecond and envisioned the police descending on his family's backyard. Digging up his missing mom. Arresting his guilty father and taking him away in handcuffs. Being sent to live with his grandparents, who, though loving, never got over the loss of their daughter.

He blinked to clear his head. This situation was different in many ways. He was old enough to make a difference now. He had authority and training to give back to society, to make amends for the cruelty of his own dad and to keep the innocent from suffering the way his mother had.

Taking a chance he wouldn't be rebuffed, he lightly touched Brooke's elbow again. As soon as she turned to look at him, he smiled slightly. "It's going to be okay. I know things look bad for you right now but as long as you're innocent you shouldn't let it get to you."

"Easy for you to say."

"Actually, it isn't," Colt countered. "It's something I had to learn the hard way. Keeping control of your emotions and exercising patience are important, Brooke. Can I call you Brooke?"

She sighed noisily. "I guess."

"Good. Think about all that's been happening, Brooke. Try to find connections or reasons why somebody is paying extra attention to you."

"Like the guy who jumped me on the trail tonight, you mean?"

"Yes. Did he say anything? Might you know him?" A

blank stare into the distant darkness indicated she was thinking, so he paused and waited for her conclusion.

Finally, she said, "I don't know why I assumed it was a man who attacked me. Now that I think about it, he wasn't very big and certainly not much stronger than I am."

"It could have been a woman, you mean?"

Brooke snorted derisively. "It could just as easily have been a teenage boy. We have plenty of those up here, although most come on spring break or during the summer. Some even get jobs working the concessions after the campgrounds open, like at the grocery or fast-food stops near the Wilderness Museum."

"How about clothing? Anything identifiable."

"Humph." Shaking her head, she explained, "Black pants, generic boots, puffy quilted jacket, gloves and a ski mask. There probably aren't more than a couple hundred outfits just like it in the park at any one time."

"That's helpful." Irony colored his words and one side of his mouth quirked.

"Ya think?"

"Yeah." Reaching for her again, he gave her arm a tug. "Come on, Brooke. We need an ID on this victim."

"And everybody just assumes I know him?"

Because she resisted he let go and brought Sampson to heel. "Sorry. Follow us."

Intent on watching her expression when she first saw the victim's face, Colt passed the crime scene quickly and stopped opposite for a clear view of the pretty ranger. Color had drained from her face except for red blotches from the cold on her cheeks and a smattering of freckles across the bridge of her nose. He had never paid attention to natural redheads before so he wasn't positive, but he suspected that such fair skin would show changes more than most.

One of the technicians kneeling in the snow was

gently brushing off the victim's face—it was a male, young-looking, with brown hair. The skin was slightly wrinkled and puckered and his lips were a sickly blue-gray color that would have told anyone he was deceased even if he hadn't been buried.

The tech leaned back on his haunches so a crime-scene photographer could snap pictures in situ, before the victim was moved. Colt kept full concentration on Brooke. Her hazel eyes widened slightly, then filled with tears.

"You know him," Colt ventured.

"No." She sniffled. "I don't."

"Then why are you upset?" It seemed like a logical question until she began to look at him as if he had just said something terrible.

"A young man has died," Brooke said. "Don't you feel the loss? The sadness that he'll never get a chance to experience the years that were stolen from him?"

"Of course, I do," Colt said quickly. "My job now is to find out who he is, who did this to him and why, and get justice."

Brooke raised an eyebrow. "While you're at it, please make sure you don't blame an innocent person, okay?"

"Meaning you?"

"Yes. Meaning me."

After what she'd seen, reality hit Brooke hard. She'd already been shaky from the cold. Now her tremulousness was coming from her core and sapping what strength she'd had left. She knew she felt ill and weak, but she didn't realize she was swaying until the K-9 cop took her arm again and started to urge her away.

Without arguing, she let him steer her toward the waiting ranger vehicles. He opened a passenger door. "Here.

Sit down before you fall down. I'll keep you posted. I promise."

"I'm okay," she insisted as a matter of course when she knew otherwise. Rangers had an image to maintain. They weren't wimps who fainted at the slightest provocation. They also didn't ask handsome K-9 cops to keep them company during crises. But, oh, she wanted to. There was a killer in the park, at her cabin, meaning anybody she encountered could be the guilty party.

Events in her past had proved difficult to face but nothing had been as bad as this. She'd dealt with being ostracized as a child because her mother had insisted on dressing her in expensive clothing and setting her apart from others in every possible way, as if having money made her better, somehow, which she knew wasn't true. Getting around that separation had been easier and easier as she'd grown older and begun making her own decisions, and by the time she'd entered ranger training she'd made up her mind to keep her familial fortune a secret.

Brooke shivered and folded her arms across her chest. Was it possible that someone knew she was one of *those* Stevenses? The obscenely rich ones. The ones who had undoubtedly made enemies via business choices. Had the person who had grabbed her on the trail meant to kidnap her for ransom?

That notion was ridiculous. Or was it? If she raised the possibility to law enforcement, she knew they would do a background search and find out just how wealthy her parents were. Then everyone would know and she'd be right back where she'd started, viewed as if she thought she was better than everybody else when that was the furthest thing from her mind. Her Christian faith had taught her that, reaffirming the conclusions she'd come to on a secular level. They were all equal in the sight of God. All loved. All forgiven and redeemed if they merely asked to be. And money had nothing to do with it, although she had often thought about how much good she could do with the inheritance that would one day be hers.

A sharp knock on the car window startled her enough to make her jump. Relief followed. It was Colt.

He opened the door halfway and leaned down to speak quietly. "The victim has been shot. Do you own a gun?"

"Yes."

"Not a duty weapon?"

"No. I'm entry-level. We do interpretive-nature talks and make sure the trails are clear, things like that."

"We'll need to take your weapon for testing."

"Of course." She glanced past him and watched a slim woman with a different K-9, a brown-and-white German shorthair pointer, starting toward the crime scene. "Who's that?"

"Willow Bates and Star," Colt said. "I've asked her to conduct a search of the grounds before we open your cabin and take a chance on disturbing the scents."

"Why not keep using Sampson? What does the other dog do that he can't?"

"Star is trained to find explosives and firearms. If a gun has been recently fired, she'll locate it."

Brooke sagged back in the seat. "Good."

"Good?"

"Yes." She chanced a slight smile. "When you find it, if you do, you can test it so you'll all know I had nothing to do with this horrible crime."

"You sound pretty convinced."

The smile spread. "Mister, I have never been so sure of anything. I'll even pray you succeed."

"You're that positive?"

Brooke nodded. "Totally."

THREE

Colt left Brooke in the parked ranger car, put Sampson in his own SUV to rest and warm up, then hurried to join Willow. "Any hits?"

"Not yet." Her concentration was on Star but she did smile. "Aren't you going to do more tracking around the perimeter?"

"Eventually. Sampson is pretty chilled. The tracks aren't going anywhere, and he needs to warm up a bit."

"Understood. If I'd thought about it I'd have brought booties for Star, just in case. She hates wearing them, though, and I think she does her best work when all she has to worry about is finding gunpowder residue."

"Yeah, my dog doesn't like them, either."

Staying in their wake and shining his flashlight ahead, he followed Willow and the pointer as they approached the burial site, then worked past it, traveling toward the cabin. He knew this K-9 well enough to tell she hadn't picked up a trail. Yet.

Willow guided Star around the far side of the cabin. There were fewer footprints evident, but there was one set that led to a small tool shed. Star pulled toward the shed and pawed at the door.

"Want me to force it?" Colt asked, directing his light toward the padlock.

"Looks like you won't have to."

She was right. The lock was in place, as if it was intact, but closer inspection showed it had already been cut.

Gloved, Colt carefully removed the lock from the hasp and slipped it into a plastic evidence bag. Then he braced himself and pushed open the door. Hinges creaked. Cobwebs hung from the low rafters. Willow gave Star the command to seek.

The well-trained K-9 wasted no time pinpointing a toolbox. Willow pulled her back and rewarded her with a pat, waiting to see if she had truly been successful.

When Colt opened the rusty red box all he saw was what anyone would expect—tools. They weren't sorted neatly, though. They were piled atop a greasy rag in the bottom. He looked to Willow. "Better radio the CSI team and get them in here. I have a bad feeling about what's under that rag."

"Me, too." She stepped outside with her dog and did as he asked.

Colt remained rooted to the spot, watching the rag as if it covered a venomous snake. If this was hiding the murder weapon, as Star thought, the pretty ranger with the innocent-looking hazel eyes was in the clear. Or was she?

He shook off his doubts. Of course she was. She'd insisted that her gun was in the cabin and, assuming she was innocent, her prints wouldn't be out here on this one. Problem solved. As soon as the techs could check her against whatever they found here, any previous suspicions would be erased.

Trading places with two white-suited evidence techs to give them room to work, Colt pointed to the suspicious toolbox and waited until they had uncovered an automatic weapon, then left to tell Brooke the news.

He was smiling when he approached and she got out of the car to meet him. "Star found a gun. Our forensics people will determine if it was recently fired. You should be in the clear as soon as they test it for prints and DNA. Oh, and we'll need to see your gun, too."

"No problem." It pleased him to see her starting to relax and even smiling slightly. "When can we go into the cabin?"

"You won't need to come along. Just tell me where you keep the gun and I'll go."

"Okay." Her smile widened and she reached into her jacket pocket. "Here's my key. I'll be so relieved when you're done. This has been a nightmare."

"Well, it's almost over." He pocketed the key ring. "They're sending a van for the body. Once there's a tech free we'll go get your gun."

"You'll have to take it, won't you?"

"Yes, but probably not keep it long. I know all this has been hard on you, but have faith."

"Do you?" she asked him.

"Do I what?"

"Have faith."

"As a matter of fact, I do. My grandparents took me to church with them."

"You do realize there's more to it than sitting in a pew on Sunday, don't you?"

He had to smile at that question. She was stuck in the middle of a mess of her own, yet nevertheless concerned about his salvation. "I do."

"Their faith convinced you?"

"No, it was much more complicated than that," Colt said honestly. "It's a long story."

"I'd like to hear it sometime," Brooke said.

Although he had no intention of telling her or anyone else about the stigma of being the son of a convicted murderer, he didn't argue. The realization that God, that Jesus, loved and accepted him regardless of his ancestry had finally brought him to his knees and changed his life for the better. However, that was personal, between him and God.

"Maybe one day," Colt said. "Get back in the car and sit tight. Where should I look for your gun?"

"It's in the back of my linen closet, behind the sheets."

He rolled his eyes. "It won't do you much good stuffed in a closet."

"Truth?" Brooke said softly.

"Please."

"I don't think I could ever shoot anybody. I just like the feeling of security I get from knowing it's there."

"You have no plans to go on into the law-enforcement side of being a ranger?"

"Nope. I'm happy right here, helping people and teaching kids how to respect the environment. I could write a book about all the funny and silly things that happen."

"Maybe someday, after you're cleared, you can tell me. Right now it looks like they're ready to go in."

"Linen closet, end of the hall, behind the sheets," Brooke reminded him.

Reluctant to leave her and not sure why, Colt started for the cabin. His mind had it all worked out. They'd find her gun, prove that it hadn't been fired, test the one from the tool shed and she'd be fully cleared.

And then what? he asked himself. The short time he'd had to spend with her had awakened the realization that his life was all work and little else. Not that he minded. He loved his job with the PNK9 Unit, everything from the training to being deployed in the field. His first choice might not have been assignment to a cadaver dog, but in a way, that felt like destiny.

It had been a dog trained like Sampson that had helped the police locate his mom's grave all those years ago. The dog had solved the crime and its instincts had ended his father's lies, once and for all. Thank God, literally, for the grandparents who'd loved him and had helped him heal. Without their unconditional love, he didn't know where he'd be or what would have become of him.

An unspoken prayer rose in his heart. It included his late mother as well as her mom and dad, then expanded to his unit members and their K-9s. The image of Brooke Stevens came to mind, making him wonder what kind of upbringing she'd had. There was something very intriguing about that park ranger, something that made him hope she'd be exonerated.

He unlocked the cabin door for the evidence team then followed them in. "Linen closet, down the hall," Colt said.

Two techs started pulling out sheets and towels and dropping them into piles on the floor. When every shelf was empty, they turned to him.

Colt gaped. "Maybe—maybe she moved it and forgot."

"You believe that?" one of them asked.

Disappointed, he shook his head. "No," he said sadly. "No, I don't."

Brooke saw Colt coming back. He did not look pleased so she climbed back out of the SUV to face him. "What's wrong?"

"No gun."

"What do you mean 'no gun'? I told you right where I keep it."

"You did. And it wasn't there."

A sense of foreboding began in her core and infused her whole body. "Of course it is." She started past him.

He stopped her physically, his hands on her upper arms. "You can't go in there."

"Why not? I know the gun is there."

"And I know it isn't."

Brooke was glad Colt was still grasping her arms because she was starting to feel woozy.

"How long has it been since you actually saw it?" he asked.

Slowly shaking her head, she tried to recall. "I don't know. I just assumed it was still there because that's where I put it."

"Was there a trigger lock on it?"

"No. I live alone. There was no reason to lock it."

"So it could have been taken today or anytime in the past." His piercing blue eyes fixed on her, and Brooke trembled at the implication.

"I'm sure I saw it as recently as last week," she insisted. "I'm always very careful when I take anything out of the linen closet because I don't want to accidentally drop it."

"You don't know a lot about guns, do you?"

"I passed a gun-safety course."

"Then you should know that modern firearms are pretty safe to handle…if you know what you're doing."

"It's a deadly weapon. I always treat it with respect."

It didn't help Brooke's mood when the K-9 cop rolled his eyes. "Anybody who's as scared of guns as you are shouldn't have one in the first place."

"Now you sound like my dad."

"He must be a smart man," Colt countered, "because I agree with him."

"Terrific." She leaned back against the side of the SUV and sighed. "What happens now?"

"They'll search the cabin, top to bottom. If they don't locate your gun, I imagine you'll be taken into custody and questioned."

"Wait a minute. I didn't shoot anybody." Brooke heard an undercurrent of panic in her tone but wasn't able to fully mask her uneasiness. Still, there were hundreds of different kinds of firearms. The chances that the murder weapon was just like hers wasn't likely.

There was only one way to find out. "Tell me more about the gun the dog found. What kind was it?"

"Automatic. I didn't stick around long enough to see the make or caliber."

Swallowing the lump in her throat, Brooke stared at him, watching his expression as she asked, "Could it have been a .357?"

"Maybe. Why?"

"You never asked me about my gun. It's a Ruger .357. The slide is really hard to pull, but I manage. I always keep the chamber empty, just in case."

He stared at her but didn't respond.

Frustration boiled over, heated from inside her by burgeoning fear. Nothing she could imagine would be nearly as bad as this whole scenario was beginning to look. "Could the gun have been a Ruger?"

"I don't know yet."

"Blued or plated?"

"It was wrapped in an oily rag but there was no silver shine so I'd have to guess blued. Even if it is the same make and model as yours, the serial numbers won't match."

"Unless somebody stole my gun."

"Yes." Sidling closer and bending to speak privately, Colt asked, "When you clean it to store it, do you wipe it down so the oil from your hands doesn't leave a residue?"

"Yes. Yes, I do." She began to feel as if a load had been

lifted. "My fingerprints won't be on it, even if it is my gun!"

"They may be on the bullets from when you loaded the clip but that would be expected. It's the outside of the gun that will tell the tale."

"Then let's go. Let's get this over with. Take me in and test me."

"That will be up to our bosses, not me. Your prints are probably on file from your background check when you became a ranger so that just leaves DNA."

"I can hardly wait."

Colt huffed. "That sounded pretty cynical. I wouldn't make fun of all this if I were you."

"You might if you were as sure as I am that I'm totally innocent. First of all, I don't believe somebody used my gun, but even if they did, the only thing I'm guilty of is not keeping it under lock and key." She paused and pressed her cold lips together into a thin line. "If that turns out to be true, then I'll accept that blame and live with it somehow. I know I was careful. There's no way I could have known a criminal would break in and steal, then kill, with my gun."

Colt tilted his head sideways and arched one eyebrow. "Sounds like you have it all figured out."

"Far from it. I just trust the workings of justice and the skill of the crime-scene techs. They can't find what isn't there."

"What if the scientific findings point to you?"

Brooke was trembling inside, yet adamant. "I don't care. I know I'm innocent."

FOUR

Willow faced Colt with a frown. "They're actually arresting her?"

"Not technically, although she will be held until she's had a second fingerprinting and a DNA test at a neutral location. Probably Ashford."

"All that can be done right here."

He had to agree. "I know. But they're playing it safe to avoid any hint of collusion. Besides, it won't hurt Brooke to be in custody for a while. She'll be protected that way."

"Humph. I'm beginning to understand exactly why Mara panicked and ran from the Stark-and-Digby murder scene last month. She looked—looks—guilty. I get that. I do. But that doesn't mean she did it."

Colt recalled the PNK9 Unit's own CSI rookie, Mara Gilmore, fleeing from the crime scene. A witness had reported seeing a woman matching her description shoot the young couple, though that witness had used a burner phone and was unreachable. But when the chief tried to reach Mara by cell phone, she didn't answer. No one had heard from her or seen her since. "I saw Mara there myself. It doesn't look good for her…" Colt stopped in midsentence. "Look, I understand that you and she were friends."

"Are friends."

"Okay. You are friends. But even people we love and admire can make mistakes. Maybe Mara let her emotions get the better of her. She was a recent ex of the murdered man. Jealousy can be a strong motivator."

"So can fear," Willow argued. "In her situation, with bullets flying and two people already lying dead, I'd probably have run away, too. Even if she witnessed Stacey Stark and Jonas Digby being murdered, that's not proof she fired the shots that killed them."

"You do have a point. I can see why she'd flee right then. Staying in hiding, however, doesn't make any sense. I don't know Mara Gilmore the way you say you do, but any sensible person would come forward to offer testimony and claim her innocence."

"Like Brooke Stevens is trying to do right now?" Willow countered. "Brooke did everything by the book except stay at the scene of her attack on the hiking trail and look where it got her."

"You don't think she's guilty, do you?"

Willow made a face. "It's just my gut instinct, but I don't think so. I do, however, suspect she's a bit too naive. I don't know how she was raised so I can't say for sure, but it's possible this is the first time she's had to face anything this serious. I don't envy her."

"If she's innocent, the evidence will clear her."

"Will it?"

Colt's jaw muscles clenched, and he took a deep breath of the icy night air. He believed in justice being served by truth. That's what had happened when his abusive father's crimes had finally been revealed.

The problem was timing, he mused. His mother's hidden grave might have gone undiscovered, and his father might have ended up unpunished, if the right K-9 hadn't been brought in and found it. If somebody hadn't gone that extra mile to solve a crime they weren't even sure existed.

So what about now? Colt asked himself. Who was going to pursue justice for Brooke? Circumstantial evidence against her was already strong and getting stronger. At this point, all he could hope was that strange fingerprints on the alleged murder weapon would clear her of firing it.

And if that didn't happen? It wasn't up to him to dig deeper into this case, he told himself. His job was to use Sampson to track and find the evidence that others would then put to good use. Right now, his first duty was to his shivering K-9 partner and he took that responsibility very seriously.

After walking Sampson back to his SUV, he ordered him to jump in, then went to work on the dog's icy feet and wet legs to dry and warm them while waiting for official release and heading back to the lodge for the night.

The big dog pressed his forehead against Colt's shoulder as if silently thanking him for the attention.

"Yeah, buddy, I'm worn out, too, but I'll take good care of you, I promise."

A solemn question immediately popped into Colt's mind. Who would be there for Brooke Stevens if the murder weapon *was* her gun and CSI found her prints on it and she was charged with murder?

Brooke had lost track of time. As the night passed, she was driven out of the park to Ashford and housed in a holding cell while waiting for the results of an expedited DNA test. Once she'd heard that the found gun was hers but that there were no identifiable fingerprints on it she was able to relax a bit.

It was one thing to *know* she was innocent and another to be able to prove it. How could she possibly prove a negative other than to provide evidence that she was else-where when that man was killed? Could anybody be sure of that timing, sure enough to give her a plausible alibi? She certainly hoped so.

One thing she did do was give in and ask permission to phone her mother the following morning, though she waited until she assumed her father would have already left for work. Her resolve was strong as she entered an empty holding cell accompanied by a deputy and it held until she heard the familiar voice of her mom. "Brooke, honey! So good to hear from you."

Suddenly, she felt like a lost child. Her voice broke when she replied, "I need help, Mom. I'm in trouble."

"I'll go get your father."

"No! He'll just rant and rave and try to bully everybody until they turn against me worse than they already are."

"Who's against you? What's going on?"

Brooke settled back on the edge of the cot in her cell and struggled to hold her cell phone steady. "It's a long story. It might be connected to the murder of a hiker found on a trail in the park last month. He'd been shot."

"What? Besides the killing of that lodge owner and her boyfriend?"

"Yes. The hiker died before them. It was kept hush-hush for the sake of tourism, and we added extra patrols for the safety of park visitors. But that was only the beginning."

Except for the occasional gasp or sigh, Brooke's mother remained quiet for the duration of the tale.

"So that's why I'm calling now," Brooke concluded. "Last night, another body was discovered buried in the snow near my cabin. My gun may have been the murder weapon. And if that's the case, it may have been used on the first victim, too."

"How many times have we told you firearms are dangerous?"

"I didn't shoot anybody, Mom. I promise."

"Of course, you didn't, sweetie. We'll get this straightened out. I'll contact our family attorneys and have them handle it. Don't say a word to anyone until you have counsel, hear?"

"It's scary. I was expecting the evidence to have cleared me by now and I'm still waiting. I keep imagining the worst."

"Are you scared enough to have prayed about it?" her mother asked.

"I must have," Brooke insisted, wondering if she actually had asked for divine help. Certainly she should have, at least when she was struggling with her attacker on the trail the night before.

Was it really less than twelve hours ago? It seemed impossible to have endured this much angst in such a short span of time. The images of that dead body, that sleeve, the wrinkled, blue hand, were seared into her memory as if they had just happened, yet were also hazy, the way a distant memory might be.

Reluctantly bidding her mother goodbye, she handed her cell phone back to the sheriff's deputy standing by to listen to her conversation. He didn't smile or offer even a small encouragement before he left her alone in the holding cell.

Alone is right, she mused, fighting back tears. It was one thing to choose independence and stand strong by choice. It was quite another to feel unjustly accused and abandoned by the very people you had called friends. That was what hurt so much. As far as she knew, none of her fellow rangers had stood up for her. The Stevens's family attorneys would step in, of course. They didn't have to believe her or even like her. They were being *paid* to defend her, so they would.

Brooke sighed, curled into a ball on the narrow cot and closed her eyes. Only God would never abandon her. Only He knew her heart. Only He could be fully trusted.

"Please, Father," she whispered in desperation. "Help me."

Colt was already up and dressed when he got a radio message from his chief, ordering him to report back to the ranger station in Mt. Rainier National Park and make himself available. He fed and walked Sampson, then met Willow outside the lodge. The sun was trying to peek between the clouds, and he hoped that meant it wouldn't rain again.

He nodded to Willow. "Morning."

"Morning. Sleep well?"

Colt quirked a smile to mirror hers. "Sampson snores."

"Awww. How sad."

"I thought so at the time." He eyed the pointer, Star. "I can see why they'd want your dog but I sure hope mine isn't deployed again. Last night was enough."

"Sampson just did what he's trained for. I'd think you'd be proud of him."

"I am."

Colt fell into step with her as they joined a group gathering in the parking lot of the Longmire ranger station, where Georgia Henning was giving instructions and assignments. She gestured at Colt and Willow. "We'll leave the cabins closest to the murder scene to the K-9 officers and their dogs. I want every dwelling visited, the occupants questioned and full reports made. My assistant will be keeping a log so nothing is missed. Any questions?"

Failing to get anything other than a murmured response, the head ranger looked to Colt and held out her cell phone to show him a map. "Your boss wants you two to interview the residents of this block of cabins. It's just to the west of the Stevens place. I don't have to tell you to make full use of your dogs, I'm sure. If you hear anything specific pertaining to the victim found yesterday I want to know about it so we can coordinate efforts. Is that clear?"

"Crystal," Colt said. He brought Sampson to heel and started off down the road with Willow and Star.

"I hear that ranger's DNA isn't back yet," Willow said.

"It shouldn't be much longer. They'll do the faster testing first and if they think they get a hit they'll go deeper. Prints were nonconclusive. That's a good sign," Colt added.

"You're still in Brooke's corner, aren't you?"

"Aren't you?" he asked.

Willow hurried to keep pace with his longer strides. "I think we should keep an open mind."

"I agree," Colt replied. "What we need to find is a witness who can clear her or, better yet, ID somebody else for the crime. We also need to hear back about connections and ballistics from the hiker found murdered in the park last month. Maybe the two crimes are linked."

Willow nodded. "Let's get on it."

They were approaching the scene of the previous night's activity, so he brought Sampson to a close heel. Movement on one of the small porches nearby caught Colt's eye. "Looks like we have a possible witness waiting for us."

"Hopefully it's more than morbid curiosity," Willow said. "I don't think I'll ever get used to folks who hang around crime scenes for fun."

Colt waved to the resident. The older man raised a coffee mug in salute and motioned them over. Stickers on the windows and a personalized license plate on an older SUV parked next to the cabin indicated that the person they were meeting had a law-enforcement background.

"I'm Officer Colt Maxwell and this is Sampson," Colt said, smiling a greeting and offering to shake hands. "My colleague is Willow Bates with Star. We're assisting the park rangers in an investigation and were wondering if you'd mind speaking with us."

"'Course not." The graying yet wiry older man shook hands with them both and Colt noted calluses on his palm. "I'm Dwight Smith, National Park Service, retired. Put in my last years in Idaho and decided to volunteer up here after that. When you've lived like this—" he gestured with a sweep of his arm "—you're spoiled for anything else."

"We're interested in the place next door," Colt said.

"'Course you are. It's not every day we have a murder up here."

"There have been several incidences of serious crimes lately," Willow said. "Did you happen to notice any unusual activity?"

Smith chuckled, coughed and took a sip from his mug. "Sure did. Can I offer you two a hot cup? I brew it a little strong, but I have plenty of milk to thin it down."

"No, thanks," Colt said. "About the Stevens cabin. What can you tell us?"

"Not much," Smith said with a shrug, "except that I watched her drag something out to the back and try to bury it. Seeing the black plastic bags made me think she was takin' out the trash, but apparently she was disposing of a body."

"You saw a woman?" Willow asked.

"Not just any woman," the witness said flatly. "Brooke Stevens. She had her uniform on and I could see that dark red hair stickin' out under her hat."

Colt was astounded. "Are you sure it was her?"

"Yup. Couldn't mistake her, freckles and all. No question. I'm positive."

FIVE

News that her DNA matched what was found on the murder weapon floored Brooke. She felt even worse when her uniform was collected for evidence and she was forced to don an orange jumpsuit.

Seeing Colt Maxwell waiting for her when she was ushered into an interview room was almost as big a surprise. She raised her hands, palms toward him, and stopped dead in her tracks. "Whoa. What are you doing here?"

"Same as you. Waiting for your attorney."

"I don't need a lawyer to tell you I'm innocent."

"Evidence says otherwise. So does your closest neighbor."

"That's impossible."

"Not according to a decorated, respected, retired park ranger. Dwight Smith saw you dragging black trash bags out behind your woodpile. He watched you go get a shovel and start digging. I imagine the ground was frozen so you settled for covering the remains with mud and snow."

"I. Did. Not." She couldn't help pacing the small, bare room. "I was at work all day. There were nature walks at ten and two and I patrolled some of the trails when I had free time. Lunch, I ate at one of the unoccupied picnic tables in the campground."

"Who saw you?"

"A family of four—mom, dad and two boys—took my two-o'clock tour. I really don't remember much about the earlier one."

"I'll need names."

"That would be a lot easier if the campgrounds were open for the season and they'd had to reserve a site. I don't ask for personal information when it's just day-trippers on a nature walk."

His phone rang. She watched him consulting it, then he frowned before he looked back at her. "Let me see your hands."

"My hands? What for?"

"Spread your fingers." She did. "Now show me the other side," he ordered.

Although Brooke obeyed, she was at a loss about the reasons. When he stepped forward and cupped her hands, one at a time, examining them closely, she almost pulled away. "What are you looking for?"

"Something that should be there and isn't," Colt said. "Are you right- or left-handed?"

"Right." Indignant, she fisted both hands on her hips. "Are you going to tell me what's going on or make me guess?"

"Calm down. One more thing." He removed his side-arm from its holster, then dropped the clip out, cleared the action and handed the empty gun to her, butt first. "Show me how you'd handle this if you were preparing to shoot someone."

"I would never…"

"Humor me. Take a shooter's stance and aim."

Brooke noticed a tremor as she pointed the gun at the blank wall. Colt circled her, peering at her hands as they gripped his gun. Finally, he nodded and reclaimed his weapon.

"Okay," he said. "That demo potentially indicates you didn't shoot this victim. What I don't get is how your blood and DNA got on the rear of the slide when there's no sign of injury to your hand and you use the proper grip. The only way you'd lose a piece of skin or bleed from firing an automatic is if you held it wrong and the ejection of the spent shell pinched the skin between your thumb and forefinger."

Examining both her hands, Brooke was relieved to see how right he was. "I told you."

"So you did."

"What now?"

"We'll give this information to your attorney, who is already here, by the way, and if your alibi about the nature walk is substantiated, chances are very good he'll be able to get you released."

"Really?"

To her delight, Colt smiled. "Yes, really."

She wanted to shout, to jump up and down, to throw her arms around his neck in celebration. She did none of those things. She did, however, start to grin so broadly that her cheeks hurt.

Eyeing her from head to toe, Colt also grinned. "Orange is definitely not your color. I hope they give you back your uniform once they've swabbed it for gunpowder residue."

"Me, too. I'd hate to have to go back to the park dressed like this even if I'm not on duty."

Chuckling, he turned to leave the interrogation room. "I'll speak to your attorney and talk to my chief. I'm sure they can work something out. Nobody goes home in a jail uniform." Pausing at the door, he knocked, and a local police officer opened it for him. "Be sure to mention that you weren't actually under arrest when we spoke just now and that you did so voluntarily, okay?"

Brooke was so relieved she chanced a wry comment. "Just be sure you wipe my fingerprints off your gun before you rob any banks with it so I don't get in more trouble."

A look of astonishment flashed across Colt's face. "Jokes? Now? Do you realize how much trouble you're in? The evidence against you is strong, Brooke."

"Oh, I get it. I just figure I can either imagine the worst and cry over it or find a way to smile in spite of it. I prefer to save my tears for true tragedy. There's plenty of that in life already. I don't have to look for it."

Colt made a face and rolled his eyes. "Have it your way. I'll have Sampson lick it clean when I get back to the car."

"Ewww. Yuck," she countered, chancing a slight smile before sobering and sighing. "Just get me out of here and find somebody to drive me home ASAP? Please?"

"If my chief gives the okay, I'll take you myself," Colt said.

"You aren't afraid to ride with me?" She was only half joking this time.

"No. I don't understand what happened or how, but you don't seem guilty to me."

"Let's hope and pray you aren't the only one who thinks that," Brooke said. "This whole mess has not been fun."

Her gaze left Colt to focus on a distinguished-looking gentleman waiting outside the door to the interview room. She recognized him from meetings in her father's office and a few dinner parties she'd attended before leaving for college. He'd been fairly young then and the last seven or eight years had been kind to him.

He shouldered past Colt and opened his arms to her. Brooke was so glad to see someone else who was on her side that she accepted the hug without hesitation. It wasn't until she stepped away a few seconds later that she noticed how quickly and totally Colt Maxwell's grin had vanished.

"It's her hands that convinced me," Colt told the PNK9 Unit chief, Donovan Fanelli, on a video call. "She'd have had to show signs of injury for a piece of skin to be stuck in the action of the murder weapon."

"Probably, although that's not conclusive."

Colt was adamant. "She claims a solid alibi for the time she was supposedly seen burying the body in the snow."

"Then explain how her DNA got on the gun."

"It was obviously stolen. She doesn't deny it was hers."

Fanelli's blue eyes narrowed as he countered, "You drive her back to the park after she's released so you'll have a good opportunity to question her in a relaxed atmosphere."

"I already suggested that."

"Good. Get her talking. Make friends with her. Whatever you need to do to uncover the truth, do it."

"I believe I already know as much of the truth as Stevens does. She's as baffled as we are."

"Are you sure?"

"Yes. Nobody is that good at pretense. Brooke didn't kill anybody." Colt saw his boss's salt-and-pepper eyebrows rise.

"Brooke?"

Colt had to smile. "Hey, you told me to make friends."

"Just now I did. Sounds like you got a head start."

"She's easy to like," Colt admitted. "There's a quality about her that makes people want to know her better."

"People, or you?"

"Everybody. The rangers I asked weren't able to give her an alibi but they did say they thought she was innocent." He paused. "Except for the retired one who happens to live next door to her."

"What did he say?"

"I haven't signed off on it yet but it should be in Willow Bates's preliminary report. When we interviewed Dwight Smith, he was positive he saw Stevens dragging a body outside and burying it."

"You just let that go?"

"Not at all. There was something suspect about the way he told his story. Willow and I agreed. He seemed delighted to be accusing a fellow ranger and that didn't sit right with us. I mean, why would a decorated retired ranger report seeing Brooke, right down to her freckles, if it wasn't true? I would have expected him to defend her."

"Not if he was convinced she was guilty."

"True." Colt sighed. "Look, she's not going anywhere as long as I'm with her and unless I'm called away on another assignment, I think you should inform Superintendent Henning that you've ordered me to shadow Brooke."

"I suppose a few days won't hurt," Fanelli said. "Just keep me in the loop. The sooner we can check the ballistics on that previous killing of the first hiker and nail down the facts, the closer we'll be to figuring this out."

"No argument there," Colt replied.

"Just watch your step, okay? You won't be the first man who let his emotions rule his good sense."

Colt huffed. "You've known me long enough to know that's not in my DNA."

"So you say. Remember, you're not your father. You don't have to let his mistakes rule your life."

Rebuttal would have been futile so Colt held his peace. He had grown up with a man whose outward appearance was so normal he could have been used to represent the perfect dad. Underneath that polished facade, however, lurked a cruelty that could erupt at a moment's notice and wreak havoc on anyone he came in contact with. To look at his father, nobody would believe he was anything but a great guy.

Shaking off bad memories, Colt nodded. "Right, so we're on the same page about Stevens? You'll let me keep her company for the next few days?"

"Yes. Just be careful."

"I will. Thanks, boss."

Colt ended the call and pocketed his phone. Sampson waited patiently at his feet, panting, drooling and looking up at him with eyes that were filled with intelligence despite the droop that gave him a perpetually sad expression. "You don't think she's one of the bad guys, either, do you old boy? Well, I agree, although it beats me how her DNA showed up the way it did."

As he returned Sampson to the rear of the silver SUV, Colt kept pondering the puzzle. He knew enough about forensics to know how immense the odds were against finding anybody whose DNA was similar to that of another person, let alone enough alike to cause mistakes. Unless...

Climbing behind the wheel, Colt contacted ranger headquarters in Mount Rainier to ask for assistance. "I have a personnel question," he told Georgia Henning. "I need to know if Brooke Stevens is an only child."

"She is," the ranger replied. "I don't have to look it up. We've talked about it. Why?"

"Just trying to eliminate all possibilities. Thanks."

"I've been told you'll be picking her up in Ashford. Is that correct?"

"Yes. I'm in Ashford now. I'll get her as soon as she's released. Have you heard if that will be soon?"

"Unfortunately, yes," Henning said. "Bring her directly to my office when you get back to the park."

"I don't think she's guilty."

"Yes, well, I didn't ask you that, did I? You do your job and I'll do mine, all right?"

"Yes, ma'am, sir." Flustered, Colt would have liked to argue Brooke's case and mention the DNA confusion but he figured this was not the right time. Every scientific answer was dependent on having accurate information upon which to base a conclusion. Even a tiny error could negatively affect the validity of findings. That had to be what had occurred in this case, although he couldn't for the life of him figure out what had gone wrong.

Approaching the jail for the second time that day, he suddenly noticed a sense of elation. Was he actually looking forward to seeing Brooke again?

"Of course, I am," he said, directing his conversation toward Sampson, as he often did when working things out in his head. "I need to ask her questions and figure out what in the world is going on."

Satisfied, Colt parked and got out, harnessed Sampson, then headed for the sheriff's office. The sooner he rejoined Brooke, the sooner they'd be able to brainstorm and hopefully arrive at some sensible conclusions.

Whispers from the hidden corners of his mind intruded before he could stop them. *What if she's guilty?*

Brooke was waiting in an outer foyer of the police station. She was so glad to see a friendly face she broke out in a grin. "Are you really my ride home?"

"I am."

"That's wonderful." She spread her arms wide. "I got my uniform back. See?"

"I take it the techs are satisfied?"

"I hope so. Nobody tells me a thing but if they'd found

traces of anything incriminating I'm pretty sure they would have kept my clothes."

"That's logical. Are you ready to go?"

"I was ready to leave before I even got here. This has not been a good day so far." It pleased her to see Colt smile slightly and arch an eyebrow at her.

"Yesterday was worse."

She rolled her eyes. "Don't remind me."

"I'm afraid I'll have to," he said, sobering. "There has to be something we're missing, some reason why your DNA showed up on the murder weapon." He paused. "And on the first victim, the hiker."

"I know. It's been driving me crazy trying to figure it out. So far I haven't come up with anything plausible. I meet a lot of folks in my job but I have no memory of coming in contact with either of those victims."

Accompanying him out the door, she felt the warmth of the sun on her face and closed her eyes for a moment to enjoy the simple gift and sigh.

Colt held the passenger door for her and she got in. As soon as he loaded Sampson, circled and slid behind the wheel, she smiled over at him. "I hate to tell you, but it smells like wet dog in here."

He chuckled as he started the engine and pulled into traffic. "Did you hear that, Sampson? Our passenger is complaining about your cologne."

Brooke laughed. "Is it his signature blend?"

"Something like that. He gets a bath pretty often but I haven't had time to spruce him up since the other night."

Hearing a reference to her troubles sobered her. "Yeah. I get that. I could use a shower myself. How about dropping me by my cabin before we check in with Georgia?"

"Sorry. Her orders were to deliver you straight to her

office." When he paused, Brooke glanced over at him. He was frowning. "Henning tells me you have no siblings."

"That's right. I'm an only child. My mom and dad are older than most of my friends' parents. They always say they're thankful they were allowed to adopt me."

Colt hit the brakes, making Brooke glad she was wearing her seat belt. By the time he'd pulled to the curb, she'd recovered. "What was that for?"

"You're adopted?"

"Yes. Why?"

"So you could have a brother or sister?"

"I suppose I could," Brooke said, staring at him. "But that doesn't matter. We'd still have different DNA."

When Colt said, "Unless you were identical twins," she felt as if she'd been plunged into an icy stream and was being held under water. *A twin?* That notion was outrageous. If she'd had a twin at birth, surely her parents wouldn't have taken only one and left the other.

"Impossible," Brooke countered. "Mom and Dad were desperate for a family. There's no way they'd have taken me and left a twin behind."

"Come up with another valid explanation and I'll listen. Otherwise, I think we should look into your birth more closely."

Open-mouthed, Brooke could only nod. No way was she a twin. She'd have known, have sensed something or someone missing from her life, wouldn't she?

As the concept whirled through her mind she began to wonder if this possibility of separation wasn't the reason for the feelings of not belonging that occasionally darkened her thoughts. That concept wasn't just unimaginable, it was unacceptable.

"I love my parents," Brooke finally said. "I don't want

to start questioning my adoption and upset them any more than I already have by being suspected of murder."

Although it took him several long minutes to respond, Colt finally said, "It will upset them a lot more if you're convicted of a crime you didn't commit."

SIX

"**R**eady for this?" Colt asked Brooke as they drove into Mount Rainier National Park via the Nisqually entrance.

She sighed before answering. "I suppose so. You said Georgia Henning is expecting me to come straight to her office, but I'd really like a clean uniform. This one doesn't look dirty but knowing it was tested gives me the creeps."

"I get that," Colt said. "I feel the same way sometimes after Sampson and I get finished. Your place is right on our way. I see no reason why you shouldn't be allowed to clean up while I wait outside."

"To keep me from running away, you mean?"

He frowned over at her. "No. Of course not. To give you privacy."

That response seemed to subdue her. "Sorry. It's been a rough couple of days. I guess I'm more on edge than I thought."

"That's understandable." He paused. "I should have asked before we passed into the park. Are you hungry?"

"A little, I suppose. I hadn't noticed."

"I always carry energy bars in my go bag. It's behind the console. Help yourself. Just be careful you get the people food, not Sampson's treats."

"They're probably better for me than a lot of sugar," Brooke quipped.

"True. But you might not care for the flavors. I'm not fond of the liver ones."

Her hazel eyes sparkled and widened. "Thanks for the tip." Beginning to peel the wrapper off one of the snack bars, she smiled over at him. "In case I haven't said so before, thanks."

"Just doing my job." And he was. There was always a sense of accomplishment when working with his K-9 and he was proud to be part of the PNK9 Unit, but having a peaceful interlude that included this particular ranger was turning out to be almost fun. In spite of her predicament and the underlying crimes that had brought them together, Colt was actually enjoying his assignment. Talk about disquieting.

"Water?" Brooke asked as she reached for a bottle.

"No, thanks. I'm good."

"Very," she teased, grinning as if she was inviting a battle of wits.

Colt was up for the challenge. "So I've been told," he quipped. "Often."

"Oh, yeah? Modest, too, aren't you?"

"It's hard to be humble when—"

Brooke interrupted, "When you're perfect. I get it."

Laughing with her, Colt kept his eyes on the road, checking the rearview mirrors out of habit, then scowled. "Are there usually a lot of park visitors this late in the day?"

"In the summer there are. With most of the campgrounds still closed until May, we don't get a lot of traffic after dark. Why?"

He shrugged. "Nothing. Just wondering. It's getting late and there are three cars coming up behind me."

Leaning to look in the side mirror, Brooke shrugged. "There are always people who think the rules don't apply to them. They get up into the park, stop at the visitor center and then pitch a fit because they aren't allowed to camp. It's actually better when our roads are closed due to snow."

"Quieter, I'm sure," Colt remarked, accelerating slightly and pulling ahead. "If I recall, there's a turnoff coming up. Hang on while I make a fast turn."

"Do you think someone is after us?"

"After you, maybe. There's only one way to check. Are we getting close to that side road?"

"Yes." Brooke pointed. "It's a left, just past the mileage sign."

"Okay. I'm going to shut off the lights. Here we go."

Colt hit the brakes. Knowing his K-9 was safely kenneled in the rear, he didn't worry about skidding to turn the corner. "Made it."

There was no dust cloud to give them away, no sign that they were being evasive once Colt turned the key and the silver SUV stopped moving.

He swiveled to look over his right shoulder. Brooke turned, too, also choosing the center of the vehicle. That put them in closer proximity than Colt was comfortable with, so he leaned away.

"I'm not going to bite you," she told him, sounding nervous in spite of her lighthearted words.

"If I was scared of you, do you think I'd have you riding beside me in the front?"

"Maybe, if it was best for Sampson."

"You've got me there," he said. "One. Two…"

"What happened to the third car? Didn't you say there were three?"

"I thought so." Colt held his breath for the long seconds it took the last car to pass by the turnoff, then released it noisily and turned back to the steering wheel. "Well, that's that. Their license plates should show up in security cameras. Once I've checked those against DMV records, we'll have a better idea of whether or not there's a real problem."

"*Real* is subjective, Colt. Those poor victims were more than real enough for me." Her eyes widened. "Uh-oh."

"What?"

She pointed behind them. "Look."

Backup lights had appeared at the side of the paved road. Brooke grabbed Colt's arm. "They *did* see us."

Although he said, "Not necessarily," he assumed otherwise. His brain was racing, along with his pulse. "Where does this road lead?"

"To a service depot."

"Is there another way out from there?"

"No," she replied, and his heart sank. The sight of a shadowy figure exiting the other car and moving into the trees for cover told him he'd have to act. Soon. There was no place to turn around and if he followed the dirt road they'd be just as trapped as they were now. Plus, the longer he delayed, the more advantage their pursuer would have.

"Hang on," Colt ordered, then started the SUV, dropped the transmission into Reverse and floored the accelerator.

Brooke braced herself with one hand against the dash, the other holding the grip bar mounted to the roof above the door.

There was a gunshot. Colt yelled, "Get down!"

Tires spun on the rough surface. The SUV rocketed backward onto the paved road, clipping the bumper of the parked car and shoving it aside as if it was a toy.

He skidded to a stop just long enough to shift into Drive. If he'd been alone he'd have taken a defensive position, radioed for backup and waited until the shooter returned to make an arrest. Having Sampson in the rear and Brooke in the front changed everything. If he lingered, he'd be endangering both of them and that was against standard operating procedure. His first duty was to protect civilians, his second was to safeguard his canine partner whenever possible and his third was to apprehend suspects. Period.

Something moved in his peripheral vision. A shadow took human form. A shooting stance. Colt stomped the accelerator and the vehicle jumped ahead with a screech of spinning tires and burning rubber.

Another gunshot sounded. Squinting at the dark road ahead, he switched on the headlights. Half-blinded, he could only hope and pray that the shooter was affected.

They were miles down the park road before he dared relax, and even then his adrenaline kept pumping.

"Did—did we lose them?"

"I think so. For now. I need to report the bumper-to-bumper collision."

"What if they follow us?"

He huffed. "I hope they do because I'll have backup then and maybe we can get a better description of the car or even a license number." Flipping on the radio as he drove, he reported the incident and gave an estimate of how soon they'd arrive.

Brooke wanted to cry, to shout, to celebrate escape and thank her rescuer. She did none of those. "Who do you think that was shooting at us?"

"I was about to ask you the same question."

"How should I know?" Hurt and a little miffed, she remained silent, trying to think of possibilities during the remainder of the trip. When Colt pulled into the yard, she noticed a distinct lack of snow. The ground had suffered so much foot traffic since she'd been gone that even the mud wasn't too bad.

She began to pat her jacket pockets, then remembered and looked over at him. "I gave you my keys."

"And I passed them to CSI. Don't you have a spare?"

"No." This was an unexpected development. "I suppose they locked up when they were done."

"That's SOP—standard operating procedure."

He started to get out so she followed. "Where are you going?"

"To check the door," Colt said.

"If it's locked, it's locked."

"Never assume."

Brooke had to jog to catch up. Colt was on the small porch by the time she reached the bottom of the steps and looked up. He grasped the knob, turned it and the door opened.

She put a hand on the railing to steady herself. "Uh-oh."

"You wait out here while I check."

Lots of arguments against his order occurred to her. She spoke none of them. What was worse, knowing there might be a prowler inside, or staying outside by herself? Neither choice was ideal so she split the difference and climbed the stairs to stand in the open doorway and watch him moving through the small cabin with his gun drawn.

As he returned to her, he was holstering the weapon. "All clear."

"That's a relief."

"I want you to walk through with me and see if you notice anything out of place or missing."

"I don't have much worth stealing."

"No more guns in your arsenal?"

"Not funny." If she hadn't been so glad to have him with her she might have told him to go away. Pride was one thing. Foolish pride was another.

Brooke glanced around the main area, which served as a living room, with a fireplace at one end and a kitchenette at the other.

The only thing she noticed missing was a framed photo of her parents holding her as a baby.

Frowning, she turned to Colt. "There was a picture on the side table by that lamp. A photograph from twenty-eight years ago."

"Of you?"

"My family."

"Okay. Anything else odd in here?"

"I don't believe so." Brooke was thinking ahead of him and hurried to her bedroom. She had to step over piles of towels and sheets at the end of the short hallway to get through the door.

Colt was right behind her. "I'll help you clean up this mess before I go."

Brooke hardly registered what he was saying. The missing picture was lying on the floor next to one she'd had on her nightstand, also of her parents. Both frames had been broken, their protective glass shattered, images ruined, as if a boot heel had been ground into them. Tears started to well. She blinked them back. Nobody had a right to violate her home this way. Nobody. What could a prowler have against her parents? A bigger question was, what did all this have to do with murdered young men and somebody taking potshots at her and Colt for no apparent reason?

"Somebody seems to have it in for your folks," Colt said pensively. "What else do you have that connects you to them?"

"Nothing, I…" Whirling, she yanked open the top drawer of her dresser and began pawing through its contents, finally tossing letters and trinkets to the floor as she eliminated them.

"What is it? What are you looking for?"

This time it was impossible to will away the tears and

a few slid down her pale cheeks. She dashed them away. "I can't believe they found it, let alone took it."

"Took what?"

Brooke drew a shuddering breath and faced him. "My diamond tennis bracelet. My parents gave it to me for my sixteenth birthday. I used to wear it all the time, even to bed, but I stopped when I got this job because I was afraid I might lose it in the forest."

"Okay. Do you have a picture of it?"

"No, but I imagine my dad had it insured."

Brooke realized how revealing her statement was when she noticed Colt's surprised reaction. "Insured?"

"Um, yes. He's always been very cautious."

"Okay. I was just wondering how much the thing was worth. I mean, insuring it seems a little extreme."

"It was a coming-of-age gift."

"And?"

"And, the links have diamonds set in them."

"And? Aren't they usually chips with shiny metal around them to make them look more impressive?"

"Some are," Brooke admitted. "Mine were actual size."

Colt was staring at her as if he either didn't grasp the significance, or was fighting to believe it. Given what he already knew, and the chance that her family fortune was behind the trouble she was having, she decided to explain.

"Have you heard of Stevens Oil?"

He nodded slowly.

"Well, that's my dad's company."

"Whoa!" Colt retreated several paces, never taking his eyes off her. "You're…"

"Rich? Yeah, by association. Dad pretty much disowned me when I chose this career." She indicated her uniform with a sweep of both arms.

"Who else knows?"

"I didn't think anybody did. Not up here and certainly not among my recent acquaintances. I walked away from it all and reinvented myself in the hopes I'd be treated like a normal person for a change. You wouldn't believe how many so-called friends were only nice to me hoping to share my lifestyle."

"You don't seem snobbish."

"Thanks a bunch." Brooke had to smile at him. "I don't suppose you have a deep, dark secret you'd like to share to keep us even."

The expression that flashed across his face reminded her of sorrow coupled with anger. Neither option was desirable so she added, "Just kidding. But I would appreciate it if you kept this conversation to yourself."

A nod was the only answer she got, but it was enough. Colt Maxwell was a principled man, one who could be trusted, although how she knew that wasn't clear. As she studied his face, she imagined myriad thoughts whirling through his mind.

Finally, he asked, "Have you considered this vendetta to be financially motivated?"

"Yes," she agreed.

"Your boss and mine should both be told."

"No. Please? I'm just getting used to feeling like a normal person. Don't spoil that."

"It goes to motive, Brooke. Think about this sensibly. Money can be a powerful incentive."

"Then why kill a stranger and plant his body by my cabin? Why not just kidnap me for ransom?"

Colt's blue eyes narrowed, darkened, reminding her of the storm clouds that often obscured the peak of Mt. Rainier. "Who says they haven't already tried?"

"When? Where?"

"When you were grabbed last night out on the trail

you were patrolling, for starters. Who knows how many other times you may have been in danger and didn't even realize it?"

"I'd have known. I'd have sensed it."

"Right, like you sensed the poor guy somebody tried to bury a few dozen yards from here."

"That's different. I wasn't even home when that happened. My boss knows I was leading tourists around during the day my nosy neighbor says he saw me doing that."

"He offered to sign an official statement," Colt countered.

"He can take an oath on a stack of Bibles if he wants to. Unless he believes in God he may as well swear on a box of graham crackers."

Colt huffed. "Sounds like you're hungry again."

"Only for the truth," Brooke said. "That's all I want."

SEVEN

Colt had reported the damage at the cabin by phone. When the call ended, he explained, "They don't have anybody else available right now and the scene was breached when we came in so the chief is leaving it to me."

"What if we were followed by that shooter?"

"Doesn't look like it to me, but we'll stay vigilant."

"Meaning, if nobody happens to be shooting at me, they don't care."

"That's a bit oversimplified. There is no reason for officers or rangers to chase an invisible criminal. If we have further contact, they're ready to come." He helped Brooke fold and replace her clean linen in the closet, then made sure she had his cell number programmed into her phone before he left to get Sampson and patrol around her cabin. He didn't envy her next appointment one bit. Georgia Henning was the kind of boss who did her job with zeal and very little compassion, unlike Donovan Fanelli, the chief of the PNK9 Unit based in Olympia. Donovan tempered his decisions with wisdom, fairness and empathy born from experience in the field. He'd even adopted his aging K-9, Sarge, when the Malinois was done serving on the force, even though there was a long waiting list of people waiting to adopt retiring police and military dogs.

Glancing down at his bloodhound, Colt smiled. "How would you like to spend your golden years with me, Sampson? Huh? Not a bad idea, is it?"

The canine responded to hearing his name with a wag of his tail. Being in his working harness meant they were on the job, but a kind word always added a spring to his step and a joyful attitude. As long as dog and handler stayed focused it wasn't against the rules.

Skirting the tool shed, Colt urged Sampson to concentrate on scents, not that that was hard to do. Bred for tracking and trained to listen to his handler, the K-9 was always eager to please his human partner. Now, he moved back and forth in a zigzag pattern, crossing and recrossing a set of boot prints that looked fresher than those from their previous visits.

The hair at the nape of Colt's neck prickled. Not only was his K-9 acting as if he'd struck a new trail, but these tracks were also newer, crisper.

Colt reached for his phone. There was nothing concrete to report so far but he thought it prudent to call and warn Brooke.

"What's the matter?" replaced her usual "hello."

"Sampson found fresh footprints. We're following them now. I want you to make sure your doors and windows are locked."

"Didn't you already check those?"

"Do it again. And close the blinds."

"Okay. Now what?"

"Now, you stay put while Sampson and I follow this trail a ways. I won't let the cabin out of my sight. I promise."

"I don't like this, Colt."

He sighed audibly. "I don't, either."

"Hurry back?"

"Just be changed and ready when I get there so we can leave ASAP."

"What if that trail keeps going? I mean, you can't just walk away without making sure any clues are protected."

"I know. I won't." That was the truth, although part of him actually hoped, for the first time in memory, that the trail would peter out and he'd have nowhere else to go but back to Brooke.

He let his K-9 continue to search while he phoned his chief and explained the changing situation.

"Well, you can't be in two places at once. Protecting the ranger should be first priority. I'll see who I can get over there to take up where you leave off. Mark the trail with evidence flags and return to Brooke Stevens."

"That's an order?"

"It is."

"Thanks, chief. I didn't want to make that call without consulting you."

Colt nevertheless remained uneasy. Since he didn't have any of the bright orange flags on his person, he left crisscrossed sticks to mark his farthest point out, then gave the fresh tracks a wide berth as he worked his way back toward the cabin.

Although he'd promised to keep her home in sight while patrolling, Colt realized that in order to avoid contaminating the new trail he'd have to cross through a gulley, then climb to the paved road. That circuitous route seemed to be taking forever.

Other than the noise from a few passing vehicles and the snuffling panting of Sampson, the forest was silent. A sense of dread overtook Colt. Made him tense. Caused him to hurry more than he already was. Sampson had apparently picked up on his mood because the big, lumbering K-9 had broken into a trot and was pulling the leash taut.

"Easy, boy," Colt cautioned. That helped some, yet the bloodhound was clearly not happy about the command.

Colt gave the leash a quick jerk. "Heel."

They crested the ridge abutting the road. Brooke's cabin was in sight again. Colt started to feel relieved when his phone rang. Caller ID told him it was her. Smiling, he pressed the icon to answer. "Almost there."

Pounding noises in the background nearly drowned out her single word: "Help!"

When the knocking had started, Brooke had naturally assumed Colt had returned. She'd had her hand on the doorknob, intending to let him in, when whoever was outside had gotten impatient and begun beating on the door.

"What's going on?" Colt demanded.

"Some idiot is trying to break down my back door."

"Hang on. I'm almost there."

She could tell by Colt's rapid breathing that he was running. Would that be enough? "So is he," Brooke yelled. "Hurry."

The sounds of heavy breathing continued, telling her without words that her would-be rescuer was giving it all he had. The person outside the door, however, was, too.

Brooke stuffed the phone into her pocket and headed for the kitchenette. She wasn't trained in knife fighting so she was not about to grab one and take the chance she'd be disarmed. An iron frying pan would have to do for defense.

It took all the courage she could muster to return to the door and place herself strategically. She raised the pan over her head using both hands and, elbows bent, stood ready to swing. The notion of causing bodily harm to anyone turned her stomach but the thought of becoming a victim like the ones they'd been finding in the park was even worse.

* * *

Colt nearly tripped over Sampson when the K-9 cut inside to round the corner at the rear of the cabin. Staggering and catching himself with his hands on the log wall, he pushed off and ran right into someone dressed like a ranger. He was about to apologize when he realized the person was also wearing a ski mask.

Sampson's leash tangled around Colt's legs just as the masked man began to kick at the K-9. Sampson yelped in pain. Colt dropped the leash to help free his dog and himself, frustrated as the thug took off into the forest.

Seeing that his K-9 was all right, Colt turned to the battered door. It was slightly ajar. Had he arrived too late after all? He straight-armed the door. It swung farther open. He started to step through.

The whiz of something big and black passing the opening startled him. It clipped his forearm. He yowled. A woman screamed. There was a heavy thud to the floor.

Recovering in a split second, he whirled and grasped Brooke's shoulders. "Stop! It's me."

A moment's struggle was followed by her going limp. He continued to steady her. "Did anybody get in?"

"N-no." Gasping for breath, her hazel eyes wide and filling with tears, she threw her arms around his neck.

Colt had no trouble deciding to embrace her, which bothered him until he thought about it. Yes, they hardly knew each other but this was a special situation. She'd been frightened, under attack, and he'd arrived in the nick of time. Reactions like these were normal under the circumstances.

Worried, Colt released her, then pushed open the door and called, "Sampson! Come."

One arm remained around Brooke. She was leaning

against him. They stepped onto the porch together in time to see the dog tugging at a scrap of cloth caught on a rough place at the corner where they'd had their encounter with the masked ranger. Head high, tail wagging, ears flapping, Sampson plodded up to them and presented the fabric.

Scolding him was out of the question. Later, under controlled conditions, they'd work on the rule to ignore evidence unless given a specific command to fetch it. Truth to tell, Colt wasn't sure his K-9 had ever been taught that in the first place, but it would make a good addition to the training protocol.

Brooke started to push away and reach for Sampson. Before Colt could stop her, she'd given the dog a pat.

Sampson sat at her feet, lowered his head and dropped the scrap on the porch.

Holding her back when she tried to pick it up, Colt said, "Don't touch that."

"Why? What is it?"

He pulled a plastic evidence bag from an inside pocket of his jacket, carefully scooped up the drool-covered scrap Sampson had dropped and held it up for examination.

"I think it's a little piece of your stalker's clothing," Colt said. "We'll be able to tell more after our CSIs check for sure, but when it dries out, I think you'll see that it's the same green as your ranger uniform."

"What are you saying?"

"The person who was beating on your door was dressed as a park ranger." He paused, thinking. "It was a woman. Actually, I thought it was your boss until I realized the person was too small to be Henning. Then, when she crashed into me and I saw her eyes, I thought for sure it was you."

Brooke let Colt handle notifications and brief the rangers who responded to her cabin. Danica Hayes, from the

PNK9 Unit, and her suspect-apprehension dog, Hutch, were with them and left immediately to follow the trail the would be assailant had made.

Colt motioned Brooke to the door. "We can leave this to my unit and your fellow rangers. It's getting late. Your boss wants to see you in her office, ASAP."

"I could have predicted that," Brooke said as he escorted her to his SUV. "At the rate things are happening to me, I'll need notes to remember the details."

"That's what debriefings are for," he reminded her. "The sooner someone is asked to recall, the less chance there is that their mind will fill in the blanks."

"Humph. There are plenty of blanks in my story, especially lately. I feel like there's a kick-me sign stuck to my back."

"More like a bull's-eye painted on your jacket."

She waited until they were both in the SUV and headed for ranger headquarters at Longmire Meadows before she continued. "Speaking of my jacket, did you give that piece of green fabric to your CSI team?"

"No, but I will. Our tech expert, Jasmin Eastwood, plans to stop by Henning's office tonight or in the morning. I'll pass custody of it to her then. It's important to keep it in our possession until I can hand it over in person."

Brooke was quick to pick up on his reference. "*Our* possession?"

Color rose in his cheeks, made plain by his blond coloring. "May as well put it that way," Colt said. "It's beginning to look as if you and I will be spending more time together."

Although she had to admit that notion sounded pretty good, she felt as if he was still seeing her as a suspect. "I'd think, now that you've seen the aftereffects of my stalker with your own eyes, you'd realize I'm the victim here."

He sighed. "What I think and what can be proven are two different things, Brooke. We still have your DNA on two victims and the murder weapon. It's impossible to set aside such solid evidence."

"I don't care what your forensic scientists say. I know I'm innocent. That's all there is to it."

"I wish that was true. I really do."

Brooke wanted him to debate with her, to at least pretend he was giving her the benefit of the doubt, but he fell silent, so she did, too.

Evening shadows lay across the parking lot at the Longmire Visitor Center which contained the ranger office. Light green leaves had begun to emerge from the hemlocks while Douglas fir and red cedar perfumed the air.

Colt parked in a spot designated for official vehicles and Brooke hurriedly got out. She paused to adjust her clean uniform and brush at invisible lint on the sleeve of her jacket. Not knowing what to expect from her by-the-book boss was causing unwarranted angst and she knew it, yet the sense of impending doom persisted.

She fell into step beside Colt as soon as he joined her. "Will you at least back up my story this time? I think everybody thought I was making it up when I reported being attacked on the hiking trail."

"Of course. So will the officers inspecting your cabin. You didn't hammer in your own door."

She quirked a smile his way. "Well, that's a relief. I know for a fact that I'm innocent and even *I* was beginning to wonder."

Together they stepped onto the raised walkway. A family—mother, father and little girl—was just leaving the Wilderness Information portion of the Longmire Visitor Center. Brooke gave them a warm smile out of habit.

They halted as if she'd put up a fence in front of them.

"You've got a lot of nerve after the way you spoke to my daughter," the mother of the group said. Her husband stepped forward protectively, his posture daring Brooke to come any closer and promising a physical rebuff if she tried.

She was taken aback. "Excuse me?"

"Don't play the innocent with us," the father said, almost shouting at her. "We all heard and saw you."

Colt took a step forward, matching the angry man's body language. "Where? When?"

"Right here, not two hours ago."

Brooke stared at the family. "Here? This morning? That's impossible."

Clutching the tearful little girl, the woman rolled her eyes and sneered. "You should be ashamed of yourself for using language like that, especially to a child. It's disgraceful. I hope they take your badge away."

Jaw gaping, Brooke looked up at Colt and saw a barely noticeable shake of his head. She felt him grasping her elbow, urging her to walk away with him. All she could think to do was keep insisting she had never spoken improperly to any child, but her accusers seemed so positive she was rendered mute.

Moisture filled her eyes and threatened to spill out. Colt increased their pace, taking her farther away from the unpleasant scene. She didn't fight him.

He stopped beside a side-door entrance to the park offices and turned her to face him. "I know how much it hurts to be unjustly accused and not be able to do anything about it, but stop and think. This was good."

The concern and empathy evident in his voice and actions was almost enough to bring more tears. "I'd never..."

"I know. They just proved your case. You were in jail until I came to get you and you've been with me ever since. Because I know exactly where you were, I also know you couldn't possibly have been the ranger those folks are complaining about. I don't know who she is, but you obviously have a look-alike wandering around this national park and we're going to find her. Brooke, I think you have to accept that you might have an identical twin you don't know about. As far-fetched as that sounds, what else makes sense?"

Brooke's jaw clenched. She couldn't think about that right now. It was both too far-fetched *and* entirely possible.

She squared her shoulders and looked into the distance to watch the unhappy family leaving. Colt was right about the run-in being a good thing. An event that could have caused her to lose her job and beloved career had, instead, proved without a doubt that she was an innocent bystander. God had truly turned something bad into something good, as the Bible promised.

Only one thing still bothered her. She couldn't have a twin. *Could* she? "Suddenly I'm not so sure I don't have an identical twin, Colt. That matching DNA had to come from somewhere."

"That's next," Colt said, pushing open the door. "Come on."

EIGHT

Colt stood back, ready to substantiate Brooke's claims, as she faced her boss. Everything he'd heard about Georgia Henning was being proven true, especially her hard-headedness.

"We can't have this repeated disturbance in the park," the head ranger said. "It gives us a bad name and keeps visitors away."

Wisely, Brooke stood at ease in front of the desk and stayed silent until asked to speak. Colt had to hand it to her. She'd snapped out of her dark mood about being unjustly accused and was now facing the verbal firing squad bravely and stoically.

"And now I'm getting reports of further unacceptable behavior on your part, Stevens. I did what I could to smooth it over but there is no excuse for using foul language, either on the job or off. You represent the National Park Service. We have a reputation to protect."

Brooke nodded. "Yes, ma'am."

"Is that all you have to say for yourself?"

"No, ma'am," Brooke said firmly. "It wasn't me. I didn't speak harshly to anyone, and I certainly didn't kill hikers or anybody else."

"One thing at a time," Henning countered.

"It's all the same problem," Brooke told her. "I was with this K-9 officer during the time when I supposedly upset that family. Since it was definitely not me, it had to be someone else, impersonating me."

The older woman pushed back her desk chair and inclined her head to one side. "Go on."

"We believe—we know for a fact there is an imposter in the park, so what's to say it wasn't her who retired ranger Dwight Smith observed digging and moving what looked like a body behind my cabin?"

"That's a reach. There's no proof of a look alike." She steepled her fingers in front of her face. "Besides, there's the matching DNA. How do you explain that?"

Brooke looked to Colt, giving him tacit permission to speak in her behalf. "I have a theory," he said, obviously choosing his words carefully. "Ranger Stevens is adopted. I suspect there may be a twin or close sibling involved. It's the only premise that fits."

"Unless you're trying to throw up a smoke screen on her behalf," Henning said. "I can see you two are becoming friends. I warn you, Officer, it will not look good on your record if you're found to be misdirecting or impeding this investigation."

"I stand on my testimony. Ranger Stevens was in custody in Ashford and then with me all morning and afternoon. There is no possible way she could be the person who used bad language to that child and her parents."

Brooke saw her boss struggling to accept his words, then beginning to relax.

"All right. Suppose I do believe you about that unhappy family. How do you propose to prove Stevens has a doppelgänger?"

"There were no DNA matches found in the federal databases," Colt said. "I think the next move should be to interview her adoptive parents and see what they know."

"She's not leaving the area."

"Then we'll do a video call, in your presence if you like."

Brooke wasn't fond of the notion of speaking to her parents in the presence of anyone else, but decided to agree in order to unearth potential clues. That was why she nodded when Henning arched an eyebrow, stared at her and said, "Whenever and wherever you choose."

"I'll have your call set up in a quiet office." She briefly consulted her computer screen, then looked back at Brooke. "We have contact phone numbers in your file. I take it they haven't changed?"

"My personal information is the same as always," Brooke said. Bile was rising in her throat and her stomach was churning. She loved her mom and dad, although, given a choice, would rather have spoken to her mother alone, as before. She knew her father loved her, in his own way. That was just the problem. His way. Things always had to be done his way.

Realizing how alike their personalities were, Brooke smiled to herself. Despite being adopted she was still B. J. Stevens's daughter, wasn't she? And although she truly hated conflict, she was going to have to stand up to him again. This time it was over more than a career choice. This time, her life might depend upon it.

The video call took place less than an hour later. Brooke was seated directly in front of the computer screen, while Colt stood behind her and Georgia Henning sat at the end of the rectangular table, listening out of sight yet close enough to move in and participate if she wished.

The middle-aged image of Jo Stevens appeared and Brooke smiled. "Hi, Mom."

Already teary-eyed, her mother started to return the greeting when her father's ruddy and wrinkled face suddenly filled the screen. "What's going on? Your mother said you needed a lawyer. What have you gotten yourself into?"

The sensation of Colt resting his hand on her shoulder and giving it a gentle squeeze helped Brooke immensely. She simply smiled. "Hi, Dad."

He wasn't placated. "Well?"

Brooke took a deep breath to help bolster self-control and spoke as if she was trying to reason with a child throwing a temper tantrum. "Well," she said calmly, "if you will sit down with Mom and let me talk, I'll explain everything as best I can."

"Where are you? Not in jail again, I hope."

"No. Not in jail. In my boss's office. With her. I—we—have some questions we need to ask you and I'd appreciate straight answers."

B.J. practically growled at the screen. "You're the one who has some explaining to do, young lady."

Brooke sensed Colt moving behind her. He appeared at her side and pulled a chair up to the table. She gave him room to join the conversation as she said, "Mom, Dad, this is Officer Colt Maxwell of the Pacific Northwest K-9 Unit. He's been investigating my case and has been very fair."

B.J. blew a huff at his computer. "Yeah, right."

Brooke wasn't going to allow anyone to speak that way to the only person she knew who was actually proving his loyalty, so she said, "Colt has been nothing but professional. I'll expect you to believe that, Dad." The grin spreading across her mother's face made Brooke proud. As always, Mom understood.

Colt spoke up. "Pleased to meet you. As Brooke has said, I've been involved in her case since my chief asked me to look into some confusing clues. I think you can help us with some answers. I know you'll want to do the best for your daughter."

It wouldn't have surprised Brooke to see her father roll his eyes and leave the conversation, but he stayed. "What clues?"

"This pertains to her adoption," Colt began.

"That's none of anybody's business." His foul mood was far from gone. Nevertheless, Brooke continued to let Colt broach the subject because her similar questions in the past had not been accepted well. Not well, at all, as she recalled. Her mother had wept, and her father had reacted as if she'd slapped his face when she'd asked for details of her birth.

"What we need to know, above all, is where she was born and if there's a chance she was a twin," Colt said.

Brooke saw her mother clamp a hand over her mouth and her father's face redden even more. He did the talking. "Of course, she's not. What kind of people do you think we are? If there were two babies we'd have taken both of them."

"Of course, you would have," Brooke said. "But there's been some DNA found that I know isn't mine and it's a match to me. There's no way that can be unless I have an identical twin."

"Somebody botched the test," her father snapped.

"There is that possibility," Brooke said. "What we—what I—would like to do is look into my adoption more closely. Surely, you can't object to that."

Her mother began to weep softly into her hands. Her father just glared at the computer screen. Brooke had one more thing to say so she steeled herself and plunged ahead.

"There is a woman up here in the park who apparently looks enough like me to fool my neighbors. We know her behavior has been giving me a bad name, but it's also possible that her DNA is what was found on a murder weapon and on two victims. There's no way I can just drop this subject the way I did before, when you asked me to not look for my birth mother."

Beside her, Colt was nodding, and he'd also placed his hand over hers as it rested on the table.

"So there you have it," Brooke said. "I will always consider you two my parents and love you dearly, but unless you want me to go to prison for terrible things that I didn't do, you have to let me investigate my past."

Her mother was nodding and sniffling into a tissue. Her father whispered something then walked away. Brooke heard a door slam.

"Mom?"

"He's gone to get your papers out of the safe. The adoption was privately arranged and he's always been afraid of discrepancies that might take you away from us."

"I'm an adult. There's no need to worry now."

"That's what I kept telling him, but you know your father. He's had attorneys look over the agreement and been assured that it's legal, but he keeps fretting about it. He does love you, you know, in his own way."

"I know."

"It's the same drive that's brought him so far in business. He thinks he has to run everything to make it turn out right. That's why he was so against your becoming a ranger. He couldn't control it for you."

"I got that," Brooke said, still anxious about what her adoption papers might reveal. "I suppose that's why you chose a private adoption."

"We were tired of wading through all the red tape involved in doing it through the state. We weren't getting any younger and were already at the top of the allowable age scale. You were such a blessing after all that time waiting and praying."

"Speaking of praying, I could use your prayers." She nudged Colt. "We both could. I can't tell you how thankful I am that somebody finally believes I could be innocent because of a solid theory."

"Sounds like you've already had part of your prayers answered," Jo said. "I do remember we had to fly to Montana at a moment's notice to get you right after you were born."

B.J. returned and slapped a manila envelope down in front of his wife. "It's all in here. If this guy is any kind of a cop he'll be able to trace you easily. I'm surprised he hasn't tried already, using your birthday."

"Those are sometimes changed when a new birth certificate is issued," Colt said. "And there would be a lot of states to check. This new information will help a lot. Thank you."

"You won't find the mother's name," B.J. said. "We never knew it. Didn't want to. Everything was handled through a small agency, and they took care of the details for us." He paused and cleared his throat. "It was all legal and aboveboard."

"I'm sure it was," Colt said calmly. "Mrs. Stevens, is there any way you could fax everything to the ranger station here or scan it and send it electronically?"

"I can scan it. I do that all the time for my quilting patterns and the charities I support," her mother said. She was sliding the papers out of the envelope and unfolding some of them.

"Good. Use Brooke's regular email and we'll print out the documents on this end."

Jo nodded, still sniffling. "I didn't remember the name

of the adoption agency but it's right here. Parkwell, in a little town called Hungry Horse. I remember landing in Kalispell and renting a car to drive over. It's beautiful country. If you'd grown up there I might think it had influenced your appreciation of nature's wonders."

Brooke smiled slightly. "Thanks, Mom. You, too, Dad. I know your hearts are in the right place. I'll let you know as soon as we find something out. I promise."

To her surprise and relief her father leaned close to the screen again and said, "We love you, Brooke." The words were familiar but this was the first time she'd heard him say them with a catch in his voice and glistening eyes. "Take care."

"I love you, too. Bye."

Filled with emotion and bathed in love, she turned her head to look at Colt. While her father's expression had surprised her, his stunned. There was so much pain in his eyes, in his countenance, that she wanted to give him another hug.

The head ranger interrupted, breaking the mood and ending Brooke's compassionate feelings. "That's it, then. Stevens, print two copies of whatever comes in your email and leave one of them with me. Mr. and Mrs. Stevens, I strongly advise you to take a vacation. Go somewhere you're not known and keep a low profile until this perpetrator is caught."

Brooke was relieved to hear her dad agree. As soon as her parents were off the computer, Henning turned to her. "You're temporarily relieved of your duties in spite of the fact that you haven't been arrested due to mitigating factors and a fancy lawyer, I was going to suspend you anyway because of the DNA evidence. This will free you to go on whatever wild-goose chases you choose."

Rather than waste time arguing, Brooke nodded politely and rose.

Colt took her hand when they left the room. At that moment, nothing would have made her pull away. Evidently, he needed her moral support as much as she needed his and that was fine with her. It was always a blessing to be able to give back, to pay it forward, as folks sometimes said.

She just hoped and prayed they weren't going to learn anything that would hurt her parents more than this mess already had. They were dear to her in spite of the fact she'd kept her background secret of late. She needed the support she knew they'd provide. There was really only them and one other person she could be certain of, Brooke thought, giving Colt's fingers a little squeeze. It didn't matter how long she'd known him or how many secrets lay beneath his professional persona, she trusted him. Completely.

Here and now, that was enough.

NINE

After taking Brooke to her damaged cabin to pick up a laptop and civilian clothes, then dropping her at one of the empty camping cabins for the night, Colt returned to his temporary quarters in the Stark Lodge. From there he emailed copies of Brooke's scanned files to his PNKU tech expert, Jasmin Eastwood. It didn't take her long to get back to him.

"Piece of cake, once I had the info you sent," she reported. "There were only three babies born in the Parkwell private clinic in Hungry Horse during that week—a boy and two girls." She paused. "The girls were identical twins."

Colt punched the air. "I knew it!"

"Don't celebrate yet. There's more."

"Go on."

"I've tried contacting Parkwell Adoption Agency. Their phone has been disconnected."

He frowned. "Disconnected? Did the agency close?"

"I can't find any information on that," she said. "Very strange." He heard her tapping on her keyboard.

"How about a trace of the owners?"

"No results yet. I'll keep trying. In a little town like Hungry Horse, the best way to locate somebody is to go there yourself. That way you can ask around and watch the re-actions of the locals instead of phoning and having to take their word for it."

Colt nodded. "I agree. I'll call Donovan and see what he thinks. Brooke Stevens is on forced leave so she'll be free to travel with me."

"As long as you're positive she's not responsible for any of the crimes we're investigating," Jasmin warned.

"I was ninety-nine percent sure even before you con-firmed she has a twin. Now, there can be no question. Her identical twin is impersonating her and doing a bang-up job of it. I just missed nabbing the imposter here in Mount Rainier."

"Then it's good you're on her trail—or the trail of the past, anyway."

"Right. Without a name or any way to track her, we'll have to go digging where she and Brooke were born for more information. Once I have a name, if you could check phone or credit card or vehicle records for me we could narrow the field a lot. Right now, we're chasing someone whose only identity has to be stolen. I know where Brooke is. Ninety percent of the time she's with me."

"What about your K-9? The chief isn't going to want you hauling poor Sampson all the way to Montana with you."

"I'll drop him off at the training center in Olympia," he said, realizing that would answer his other concern, too. "He needs a break and I want the vet to check him over for injuries. He's acting okay but he took a couple of hard kicks in the ribs."

"Poor guy. Those three bloodhound pups gifted to the PNK9 Unit and going through training are sure cute. I hope he doesn't think you're trading him in on a new model."

"Never happen. He and I are perfect together." Colt

chuckled. "Most of the time. He did slobber all over a piece of evidence before I could tell him 'leave it.'"

"Evidence?"

Colt glanced at his coat. "It looks like a piece of fabric torn from a park ranger's uniform. With Sampson's drool all over it, I doubt there's any salvageable DNA but I bagged it, anyway. I'll bring it with me when I stop by headquarters."

"Do you want me to see about getting you a chopper or will you drive over?"

"I'd rather fly. It's quicker. I'll need to clear it with Donovan and arrange for Brooke to accompany me so I'm not sure of the time."

"Okay. Just be careful. I don't know what's going on but too many people are turning up dead."

"*One* is too many," Colt said firmly, and his thoughts immediately added, *like my mother.*

Brooke made do with the standard amenities in the rental cabin and the personal things she'd picked at her place. As she changed into jeans, a long-sleeve shirt and her work boots, she wondered if she'd be allowed to go home once they got the broken door repaired. Only if she still had a job, and that depended upon locating and capturing whoever was leaving identical DNA behind. A twin! An *identical* twin. Who would have thought it?

The notion of pursuing and apprehending a person who looked just like her, who shared her DNA, who had the same birth parents, was hard to process. The concept was bizarre. Little wonder Henning and others didn't want to accept her innocence without proof. If she'd been in their shoes she would have doubted, too.

Brooke was startled by a knock on her door. "Who is it?"

"Me. Colt. And Sampson."

Relief flooded her. Struggling to calm her jumpy nerves, she answered the door. "Whew. I was afraid it was my stalker."

Stepping back, she gestured for them to enter. "Come on in. Both of you."

"Thanks." Colt was eyeing her from head to toe as if they had never met.

She scowled. "What?"

"Nothing. I've just never seen you wear anything but your uniform and that ugly jumpsuit."

"It feels kind of strange to me, too. Anything that isn't green seems wrong, you know?"

Grinning, he held out his free arm to display his own shade of green via his official PNK9 Unit jacket. "I do."

"What brings you by so early?"

"We need to make plans, and I thought it was better to talk it over face-to-face."

"Gotcha. I found some coffee and brewed a pot. Can I offer you a cup?"

"Please." Colt kept Sampson at heel, in spite of the fact the K-9 wasn't wearing his working vest, and went to the small table next to the makeshift kitchen.

Brooke was glad he let her hand him the mug of steaming coffee before he said, "My tech expert hasn't been able to reach the adoption agency your parents used. Their phone's been disconnected."

She plopped into the only other chair and leaned her elbows on the table. "Oh, dear."

"Is that all you have to say?"

Brooke almost laughed. She did smile. "Haven't you heard? I save all the colorful language for small children and park visitors."

"Yeah. Good thing you were with me when that happened."

"Very good. I might even say it was providential."

"Maybe it was." He paused to carefully sip from the mug. "And maybe there's more to come—at least, I hope there is. I've spoken with my chief. He's arranged for a helicopter to pick us up and fly us to Hungry Horse to have a look around. It's possible we'll be able to turn up the people who run—or used to run—the adoption agency."

"Do you really think so?" There was no way she could hide her enthusiasm.

"No way to tell unless we try."

"Will I need to pack a bag?"

"I assume it will be a day trip by chopper, but it wouldn't hurt to bring a few things. We'll be stopping by the training center at Olympia so I can drop off Sampson for some R and R."

She heard the K-9's heavy tail thumping on the floor when he heard his name. "Too bad you can't take him along."

"Not this time. He needs a break and I want the unit vet to give him a health check."

That was worrisome. "He's okay, isn't he?"

"I think so. Just playing it safe. And it'll be a good opportunity for me to show you around my base of operations."

"I'd love that. When do you want to leave?"

"Ten minutes ago," Colt quipped. "We can grab breakfast on the way to the helipad."

Although she tried to mask her apprehension, Brooke's hands trembled slightly as she carried her mug to the sink.

Colt noticed. "Are you okay?"

"Sure. I've always wanted to hang in the air on a little, thin propeller and shoot up through the trees into the clouds. Whoopee."

"Not a fan of flying?"

"Not a fan of leaving solid ground, truth be told. If God had wanted man to fly, He'd have given him wings."

Colt laughed. "He gave us the brains to build airplanes instead. It's not like I'm asking you to become a test pilot." He continued to chuckle and grin. "Sampson's not a bit scared."

"Sampson is a big, goofy, drooling creature with ears bigger than my feet and feet as big as my fist." She started to reach to pat the dog's broad head. "He's out of uniform so it's okay to give him affection, right?"

"This time, I guess. Just don't get too attached. He's supposed to be bonded with me."

Brooke had already bent to cup the huge head in her hands, ears and all, and was looking deeply into the bloodhound's eyes. "It's as if he understands my thoughts." She looked to Colt. "Do you get the same feeling?"

"Yes, I do." Color infused his cheeks, as if he was embarrassed, then he laughed and added, "Makes me really glad he can't talk."

The morning mist was thick and clouds encircled the peak of Mount Rainier as Colt piloted his SUV toward the Nisqually exit of the park and the small airport where they were to board the helicopter.

"It's so beautiful up here," Brooke said dreamily.

"I like it better when the fog lifts and the sun comes out. It's safer driving, too."

"True." She passed him a take-out cup of coffee. "Here you go. No cream and two sugars. Let me know when you want your breakfast sandwich."

"We should have half an hour or so while we wait for our ride," Colt said. "I'll eat then."

"Okay."

Seeing her close the take-out bag and set it aside, he

smiled. "That doesn't mean you have to wait. Go ahead. Enjoy."

"You're sure? I don't want you to feel left out like your poor, starving dog back there."

"He'll live. He had his usual big breakfast before I left the lodge this morning."

"Why didn't you eat then?" Brooke asked.

Colt shrugged, sensing his cheeks warming again and ruing his blond coloring. "I thought I'd wait and share a meal with you. You don't mind, do you?"

"Not at all." She unwrapped one of the identical sandwiches and took a bite. "This is really good. Are you sure you don't want a taste before it gets cold? I can hold it for you."

Instead of waiting for his reply, she unwrapped the second sandwich enough to expose half of it, folded back the paper and swiveled to face him. "Here you go. Bite."

"*Not* while I'm driving." Colt knew his response was abrupt and perhaps too harsh-sounding, but he'd spotted something odd in his rearview mirrors and didn't want to be distracted.

"Okay, okay. Sorry."

The way she shrank back in the passenger seat and averted her gaze told him he'd hurt her feelings. That bothered him, but he had no time to apologize.

He took a few seconds to recheck traffic behind them, then explained, "I didn't want to worry you, Brooke, but I think we're being followed."

"What?" Her head snapped around. "Where? Who?"

"I don't know for sure. Besides the fact that we're not supposed to do anything but drive when we're behind the wheel, I didn't want to be distracted by eating, just in case."

"Just in case what?" The sandwiches were already

stowed and she was evidently looking for a secure place to put her hot coffee.

"In case it's necessary to try to lose our tail."

"On these roads? There's no place to go except straight ahead."

He had to agree. "These low clouds don't help, either. Even if I knew this road by heart it would be foolish to speed."

"What are we going to do?"

"Stay safe." Which was Colt's goal at all times, especially when transporting his K-9 partner. Adding another human, particularly Brooke Stevens, to the equation increased his problems exponentially.

Clutching the steering wheel tightly, he accelerated. All four tires gripped the damp pavement. Much of the road meandered through a forest. It was the part that ran along the sides of the mountain and included drop-offs and cliffs that worried him most.

Just when Colt was ready to take a deep breath and consider them in the clear, more fog appeared. Shady sides of the canyons were cooler and held the moisture suspended until sunlight finally dissipated it later in the day. He'd traveled roads like this before but never moving this fast unless responding to an active crime scene, and never with passengers, human or canine.

The engine continued to roar as he backed off the gas. "I just want to get to Ashford," Colt shouted across to Brooke. "Make sure your belt is tight."

She was peering in the passenger-side mirror and the pitch of her voice was higher than normal. "What do you see?"

Another looping curve appeared out of the fog. Colt steered into it expertly, even when it immediately turned back on itself. That's when he again saw the vehicle behind them. A large box truck was negotiating the first part of the snakelike turn. If it wasn't chasing them, its driver was unhinged because he was barely keeping the truck on the road.

"Look now," Colt countered, inclining his head to point.

"That truck?"

"Yes."

"It's probably okay. They deliver groceries up here all the time," Brooke said, sounding hopeful.

Colt wasn't about to slow down. Not with the truck gaining on them. "Do they always drive as though they have no brakes?"

"No, but…"

Colt wasn't about to rely on her misplaced complacency. "You can ask the driver the next time you see him. Or her. Right now, I'm busy getting out of the way."

"These roads are dangerous enough on a good day. Stop and let me out if you're going to drive like you think you're on a racetrack."

"Seriously?"

Brooke made a wry face. "No."

He glanced in the mirror just as the truck's headlights showed that it was rounding the second half of the *S* curve. "Too late for that, anyway. Here he comes. Hang on!"

TEN

Brooke wanted to scream and would have if she hadn't feared startling Colt and causing him to make an error. She could see the delivery truck pretty clearly in her side mirror when their SUV turned to the right. Other times, it seemed to disappear.

There was no place to get on her knees and pray so she simply cast her eyes to the sky as she looked through the windshield and called silently for God to rescue them. Instead of cessation of the chase, however, the larger truck clipped the rear bumper of Colt's SUV.

It shimmied. He corrected and kept it on the road.

"Did they just ram us?" Brooke yelled.

"Felt like it."

Managing to turn in her seat enough to look out the rear window, past the specially constructed compartment designed to keep Sampson safe, she caught a glimpse of something that stole her breath. She gasped, then clapped a hand over her mouth.

"What is it? What do you see?"

"That driver. It's a woman, and she looks exactly like me. It's like a bad photo."

"Is she alone?"

"I think so." Brooke sensed the SUV slowing. "What are you doing?"

"Arresting her as soon as I find a place to pull over. I'm armed. There's no reason to keep running away if she doesn't have any backup."

A sense of dread flowed over and through Brooke, making her shiver. "Be careful."

"Always."

"Yeah, well…"

"You just stay in the car with Sampson while I deal with your look-alike, okay? I can handle this."

She wanted to believe him, wanted to tell him she had complete confidence in his abilities, and she did, with reservations. There was cunning and dangerously twisted thinking involved here. Anybody who could go around killing innocent people couldn't be dealt with rationally or predictably. That was what Colt needed to keep in mind.

"Look, just because this woman looks like me and has the same DNA, don't be fooled," Brooke warned. "We know she's not the same. Not one bit."

Colt glanced over at her and took his eyes off the road for a mere instant.

From the corner of her eye, Brooke saw the truck looming behind them. "Look out!"

His reactions were not quite fast enough. The truck hit them on one side of the rear bumper and sent the SUV careening into the cliffside. Metal crunched, folded, tore. The tires began to slide as Colt tried to correct their course. Then, they were airborne.

Tree branches and wet vegetation slapped against the windshield, obliterating the view. Brooke raised her arms to protect her face. Glass shattered into spiderweb patterns.

"Colt!"

In the brief seconds it took for the trees and plants to

halt the SUV's descent, he didn't answer. Images flashed through Brooke's mind but she wasn't reviewing her life, she was picturing what might lie ahead and it wasn't pretty.

Then it was over. They stopped moving. Colt turned the key and without the engine noise, the silence was startling. So was the fact that they hadn't plunged all the way to the bottom of the canyon. Stalwart firs had saved them.

Brooke started to reach for the door handle. Colt stopped her and said sharply, "No. Don't move. I'll call for help."

"What if she comes back?"

"We'll see her if she does. Right now she probably thinks she finished us." Colt eased off his seat belt so he could turn enough to check on Sampson.

Brooke was concerned, too. "Is he okay?"

"Yes. The traveling compartment protected him much better than a crate would have."

"That's a relief." She listened as he radioed for assistance and gave their GPS coordinates. Behind her, in the area constructed specifically for K-9 transport, she could hear Sampson panting. He was also pacing back and forth as much as the small space allowed.

The vehicle shuddered. Jerked. Moved enough to slip past one of the Douglas firs and start to slue sideways.

Brooke gasped. One look at Colt told her he was just as concerned. Again, she reached for the handle of her door. This time, he nodded. "Slowly. Move as little as possible and ease it open. Don't let it fall forward."

Every nerve in her body was firing. Tremors shook her in spite of an immense effort at self-control. As soon as she opened the door as far as it could go, she looked to Colt. "What about you?"

"This side of the car is caved in. I'm not sure the doors will work. I want you to slide out and get clear before I try my side."

"What about Sampson?"

Colt pressed a button on his key fob and when a panel between the front and back seats lifted, he blocked the exit with his hand. "You first," he said to Brooke. "When you're clear, I'll release him. I want you to call him to you and grab his collar for me."

"Okay. Now?"

"Yes."

The mere effort to swing her feet around and out the open door caused the SUV to shift again. She froze, waiting. When she was convinced it wouldn't go any farther, she pushed off and stood.

The slope was steep and the ground foliage was so wet with dew and fog that her feet slipped. Dropping to her knees on purpose, Brooke began to crawl away, getting better purchase by grabbing fists full of plant material to pull herself along. Reaching a hemlock sapling, she used it to help her stand and turned back to face the tilted SUV.

"All right. I'm clear," she called.

The tan blur of a galloping bloodhound came straight up the slope. Sampson circled her and the small tree she was holding on to, then plopped at her feet, looking quite pleased with himself.

"We're okay. C'mon," she called to Colt.

Slight movement inside the SUV was followed immediately by another shudder and further descent of at least a foot. The tires were tearing swaths in the tender ferns and mosses, leaving tracks in the mud and loose rocks below them.

Brooke caught her breath. Fervent prayer was easy. "No, no, no. Please, God, no."

The SUV jerked again and slid another few inches sideways. In the distance, she could hear sirens. That would have been a lot more comforting if her friend and rescuer was not still in such a precarious position.

"Help is almost here," she shouted, knowing that Colt's rescue could come too late and wondering why the thought of anything happening to him felt like a knife to her heart. Of course, she cared—she cared for all people, she argued, hoping to circumvent the growing realization that this particular man was so special to her. They hardly knew each other and yet her feelings were honest. And strong. And undeniable.

Holding tight to Sampson's collar with one hand and the sapling with the other, she asked God to protect Colt with all the faith and all the fervor she could manage. He did matter to her, more than she would have suspected if she hadn't been afraid she was about to watch him fall to his death.

"He can't die, Father. Please, Jesus, help him," she whispered into the blanket of fog.

Sampson picked up on her mood, quieted and leaned his big body against her legs as if offering solace.

Brooke placed a hand on his broad head, closed her eyes and kept praying.

The shuddering of the SUV unnerved Colt enough to slow his movements even more. Without Brooke and the heavy dog, the balance was different than it had been when they'd been forced off the road. His task now was to preserve his own life.

"Not losing this expensive vehicle would be nice, too," he muttered to himself, wondering if Chief Fanelli had heard about the accident yet. Chances of apprehending the driver of the truck responsible were slight, particularly once she reached a town. If he had been the criminal behind the wheel, he'd have abandoned it as soon as he could and disappeared.

It was hard to picture a woman who looked exactly like Brooke being an assailant, yet he was sitting here in the proof, wishing he could get out and wondering how much more effort he dared use.

The center console contained both radio equipment and his computer system, making it difficult to climb over unless you happened to be a K-9. Oh, he could do it if he had to—he just couldn't help wondering if the attempt would make the car even less stable.

Unsure, he slid the driver's seat as far back as it would go and unfastened his safety belt. With one hand on the door handle, he released the catch, then pushed out with his shoulder. Nothing moved. Nothing gave. That door was wedged tight, as he'd suspected, and because of the inward dent, the power window refused to budge, too.

That left only one way out, if he chose to take it. As long as Brooke and Sampson were safe, he knew the smartest thing to do was sit tight and wait for first responders to secure his vehicle with a cable so it didn't slide any farther down the steep slope.

Sounds of distant sirens reinforced his decision to stay where he was, while the urge to be closer to Brooke nagged at him like a dog gnawing at a bone. For the sake of his nerves, he called to her. "Are you still okay?"

"Yes," she replied, but her response sounded feeble and unsure, so he shifted a little more to try to see her.

"Are you sure?"

This time, she didn't reply. She did, however, enter his field of vision. Her shoulders were slumped and she was backing into a copse of ferns, dragging Sampson behind her. "Brooke?"

Raising her free hand, she pressed her index finger

vertically across her lips, shook her head and kept inching back until all he could see was the occasional wag of Sampson's tan-colored tail.

The only reason for her to be acting like that was fear and that emotion seemed to be so strong it was almost palpable. What was keeping those rescuers? He could still hear their sirens, but the hills and valleys of the mountainous region distorted sound so much there was no way to tell how close they were.

He grabbed the mic from the console. "Units responding to accident scene near Longmire, be advised, one of the parties involved may be armed and dangerous."

"Copy" was repeated twice.

"Probable ETA?" Colt asked.

The soonest estimate was five minutes. That might be too long, particularly if Brooke's evasive actions had been observed by whoever had been trying to ruin her life.

That left Colt only two choices, one of which he immediately discarded. No way was he going to just sit there and wait for a killer to strike. Therefore, getting out of his vehicle and assuming a defensive position was necessary. Because Brooke was hiding and because he couldn't see the roadway above them, he would have to exit quickly and take cover to assess the situation.

He closed the computer, pushed stationary equipment as far out of the way as possible, then drew his legs under him, ready to leap if necessary. His sidearm had to remain safely holstered until he was done clambering over the seat and out the door, which meant he would be vulnerable for several seconds. That couldn't be helped.

Taking a deep breath and tightening every muscle, he put one hand on the dash, the other on the back of the passenger seat and started to move toward the door Brooke had left open.

A shot echoed!

Colt ducked but kept moving, then hit the ground and rolled away, hoping to make a poor target.

Movement on the road above lasted for a mere instant, but he caught it in his peripheral vision. Crouching, he drew his gun and aimed it at the rock berm they had bounced across when they'd left the road.

Nothing was moving. Patches of fog shrouded the forest and water dripped from new spring leaves as if the trees were weeping. Listening for anything that would prove Brooke was uninjured, he finally heard his K-9 panting.

On the road above, an engine started and revved, the sound fading as if it was moving away.

Colt straightened slightly and called, "Brooke? Are you okay?"

The lack of a reply was unnerving until she showed herself to him and raised a hand.

"The dog?"

Again, she waved. This time she nodded.

"Was that shot anywhere near you?" Colt asked. He was already on the move toward her.

She pointed at the wrecked SUV. "Back window."

The last few yards disappeared beneath his boots as he holstered his gun. Momentum carried them both into the foliage, where branches and fronds closed around them in a blanket of green that provided temporary respite. Nothing could have stopped Colt from taking this woman in his arms at that moment, not even a new threat. Something about her insisted that he protect her however he could, even with his own body if there was no other method available.

Truth to tell, once he was holding her close he realized he needed the mutual hug as much or more than she did. For the first time since his teens, when his mother's grave had been found, he was blinking back unshed tears. The sensation should have been embarrassing. Instead, it almost felt cleansing, as if this moment could surpass or even erase past pain.

Without thinking, Colt lowered his head and placed a tender kiss on Brooke's silky auburn hair.

ELEVEN

On the road above, emergency responders were stopping and gathering. Someone with a bullhorn stepped to the edge and boomed, "Scene is secure. Any injuries?"

Colt eased away from his trembling companion, took her hand and led her and Sampson into the open while keying his radio. "All good down here. Watch out for a grocery delivery truck. The driver is armed and dangerous."

"Nobody here but us," the man with the bullhorn replied. "We're sending medics down to you on ropes. They'll help you climb up to us."

Turning to Brooke, he smiled. "You go first. I'll follow as soon as they secure the vehicle and I can get my gear."

"I—I don't want to leave you."

Colt's expression widened to a grin. "Same here. But if we want to avoid starting more rumors I suggest you play this by the book. When and if we ever get to Montana to check that adoption agency, we can be less formal."

"I'm not in uniform. I should be allowed to act like everybody else."

Colt shrugged. "Maybe. But I'm on duty and so is Sampson until I drop him at the training center."

A twinkle in Brooke's pretty hazel eyes surprised him enough to cause him to arch an eyebrow. When she joked,

"I suppose this means you don't want me to throw myself at you again," he chuckled.

"Well…" It was to her credit that she was able to joke around after the scare they'd had. He, for one, often used humor to defuse tense situations. It was just odd to be met with a similar tactic. Odd and rather comforting.

Brooke laughed. "Don't worry, Colt. I won't embarrass you, and as you said before, your K-9 can't talk so he won't tell tales."

"The hug wasn't all that bad," Colt said with a lopsided smile. "I mean, if you felt the necessity to celebrate survival *again* I could probably be convinced to repeat it."

"I'll keep that in mind." A rescuer wearing a bright orange vest and harness fastened to ropes was backing down the slope toward them, the way a climber would rappel off a cliff. "Looks like my ride is here."

"Looks like it." Loathe to let her go, he nevertheless helped the rescuer strap her into the dual harness then stepped back as they left to start the climb.

Watching Brooke go was a lot harder than Colt had imagined it would be. He wanted to clamber up the slippery, uneven slope barehanded just to stick closer to her.

Sampson nosed him for attention and got it. "I haven't forgotten you, boy. Let me check you over again while we wait."

The dog stood stoically while Colt inspected every inch of his furry body from head to tail and pronounced him in perfect shape. That was more than he could say for the official SUV. It didn't look totaled, but it was far from the shiny silver vehicle he'd started with that morning.

Pulling out his cell phone, he was delighted to see that it was undamaged. Finding more than one tiny bar made it difficult, but he managed to call his chief by testing the signal strength in various areas around the crash site.

Donovan answered immediately. "You okay? The dog?"

"Yes, and the ranger I was driving to the helipad is uninjured, too." Pausing, Colt gave his chief the opportunity to ask more questions. When he didn't, Colt took the initiative. "I may need to borrow one of the other unit vehicles while mine is in the shop for repairs."

"So I'd gathered from the dispatches. How bad is it?"

"Nobody died," Colt quipped, knowing his friend wouldn't mind a little dark levity, considering.

"That's a plus," Chief Fanelli said.

"I thought so. It'll be a while before I'm done here. Would it be okay with you if we delayed that flight to Montana? I'd like to spend a full day in Hungry Horse."

"Logical. Stevens is okay with that?"

"I haven't asked her," Colt said, "but she'll go along with whatever you and I decide. She's really eager to find out more about her twin."

"You're convinced that's what's going on? You're positive it's not her?"

"I didn't need any more convincing. After this morning, even the biggest doubters would change their opinions. We saw her, Brooke and I. She was driving the delivery truck that shoved us off the road."

"There's no mistake?"

Colt huffed as he watched rescuers at the top of the slope helping Brooke out of the dual harness. Looking back at him, she waved. "No mistake," Colt said firmly. "I've never met a more innocent suspect in my entire career."

"All right. I've alerted local law enforcement in Ashford and beyond, just in case. If the twin is as smart as we think, she'll abandon the stolen truck and maybe we can get a good set of prints off it."

"Affirmative."

"As soon as you get everything settled there and make

sure Stevens is safe, I want you to get back here and interview Eli Ballard again." Colt pictured the man who'd been murder victim Stacey Stark's business partner and good friend. Ballard was now running the three Stark Lodges on his own until Stacey's brother, who'd inherited her share, decided how he wanted to proceed. "Eli's apparently uncovered some new information about the owners of competing lodges using unfair business tactics and we can't lose focus regarding the Stark-Digby murder case, especially not with one of our own a person of interest."

For the second time recently, Colt pictured Mara Gilmore, their rookie CSI, when she ran from the scene of the double homicide. He shook his head. "This must be so hard on Asher," Colt reminded the chief. Mara's half brother, also an officer with the PNK9 Unit, was a good friend of Colt's.

"Not as hard as it would be if he'd grown up closer to his half sister."

"True. Still, there is a family connection."

"Not a solid one," Donovan replied. "If Mara and Asher had been close before she was spotted fleeing that murder scene, I might have to put him on leave. Thankfully, that's not necessary."

"Willow insists Mara is innocent."

"Yes, but they're good friends. I'd agree if you and Danica hadn't spotted her at the scene of the double murder and watched her run away." He paused, then added, "If she wasn't guilty of *something* she'd have gotten in touch with me or turned herself in by now."

"That does seem likely."

Colt had been watching rescuers attach a steel cable to the rear of his damaged vehicle. They stepped clear, radioed to the tow truck on the road above and the silver SUV started to move, creaking and groaning as they pulled it free. "Listen, I'm about to need both hands to climb out of this canyon. I'll check in with you as soon as I get a damage estimate on the car."

"Right. Let me know when you want the chopper back and where you want to be picked up. In the meantime, do the best you can to hitch rides with the park service. I've spoken to the head ranger at Mount Rainier and she's agreed to provide temporary transportation."

Colt snorted a chuckle. "Georgia Henning? I imagine that conversation was memorable. She's pretty hard-headed."

"Ya think?" The chief laughed softly. "Not too fond of your friend Brooke, either, by the sound of it."

"She *is* my friend," Colt admitted without reservation. "I really have to admire her for keeping it together when so much evidence pointed to her."

"Until you locate that supposed twin and have her in custody, Stevens is still a likely suspect. You do understand that, don't you?"

"I do. But I have no doubt Brooke is totally uninvolved in any of the crimes she's been accused of."

"The neighbor who reported seeing her burying that body could have easily seen her identical twin."

"Exactly. When two people look so much alike, anybody can make a mistake."

Donovan sighed. "Just remember that applies to you, too, Colt. Don't get too close to a suspect and let that influence you. Follow the evidence as faithfully as our dogs follow a trail and don't go off chasing rabbits, if you know what I mean."

"I do. I'm not going to let a pretty face sway me."

"An identical twin can be a tricky situation. Don't let your guard down no matter what."

"Like I did this morning?"

"Hey, I never said that. We'll let CSI decide what happened to make you lose control. Those mountain roads are treacherous in the best of weather, and I understand it's foggy up there."

"It was. It is. Wet and slippery, too. But that's not why we left the road. We were hit. Hard. There should be plenty of evidence of paint transfer." Colt watched the SUV finish its trip and crest the berm.

"Plan a quick stop in my office when you're dropping Sampson off or picking him up. You can tell me all about it in person."

Colt grimaced at the phone. "Yeah. That's what I was afraid you'd say."

Brooke broke into a wide grin and hurried forward as soon as she saw Colt finish his climb. Sampson was with him, panting and wagging his tail as if they were playing a wonderful game. Colt didn't look half as pleased. She understood when she followed his line of sight to the flatbed wrecker that was winching his wrecked SUV onto its platform.

She fell into step beside him. "The ambulance guys want to check you over, too."

"In a minute." Leaning in, he was peering at the rear bumper. He pointed. His mood brightened. "There. I knew it. We were hit and pushed off the road. There's the proof."

"Are the police outside the park looking for the truck and the other driver, too?"

"Yes."

"They should use my picture," she said. "We saw how much she looks like me."

"That's another reason for you and I to stay together," Colt warned. "I don't want to be escorting you out of jail again."

"Fat chance," Brooke said, unable to squelch the smile she'd had ever since Colt had rejoined her. "You'd have to take a taxi."

"My boss wants to see me at his office once we get that chopper ride."

"Olympia, right?"

"Yes."

Brooke didn't fault him for continuing to examine the wreck instead of paying more attention to her. After all, it was her fault in a twisted, obscure way. If she hadn't been his passenger, her look-alike wouldn't have attacked. When she'd heard from Colt that the young couple killed in the park last month did not have her DNA anywhere on them and the ballistics report proved the gun used wasn't hers, she'd been immensely relieved.

Her shoulders sagged, her smile fading. "I wish…"

"What? What do you wish?" Colt asked.

"I'm really not sure," she said honestly. "Maybe that I'd known sooner. It's hard to wrap my mind around having a sibling."

"There doesn't seem to be any other explanation, especially considering the DNA. You're better off proving you are a twin than having no plausible excuse for the clues left behind. If it's not her, it's you, and I know better than that."

"Thanks." Pensive, Brooke followed Colt as he left the wrecker and headed toward the ranger vehicles. "The whole thing may make sense to somebody else but it sure doesn't to me," she said. "I mean, first she kills young men I don't know, then she tries to kill me. At least that's how it looks. Why?"

"I don't know. Maybe she doesn't know, either. Maybe she's just mentally ill."

"And as her identical twin I should be too, right?"

"Not necessarily. There's nature versus nurture. I did a

little research online when this idea first occurred to me and found out that even what's called identical twinning isn't exact. Only about ten percent are genetically the same. The rest differ in some way through mutations in embryonic development. If the change occurs early, the differences are more pronounced by the time the child is born."

"So my sister and I, whoever she is, are in the minority."

"In more ways than one," Colt told her. "Look, don't borrow trouble by worrying about it ahead of time. We'll track her down and sort all this out. I promise."

Brooke arched her eyebrows and rolled her eyes. "I appreciate your help, really I do, but I'm starting to think that hanging around with me can be detrimental to your health." She glanced toward the tow truck. "Case in point."

"Just doing my job."

"I thought your job and Sampson's was locating cadavers. It's not very comforting to hear you say I'm your job."

"For the present, my chief has asked me to help solve several crimes, including the earlier murders of Stacey Stark and her boyfriend, Jonas Digby. That keeps me busy here in the park and if there's nothing else for me to do in my spare time, I may as well work on your case, too."

Brooke cast him a lopsided grin. "I get it. I'm busywork to keep you out of mischief."

The look of astonishment on Colt's face was so comical she had to laugh. "Just kidding. Sort of."

"Thanks for clearing that up. I thought you were serious. I really do…"

When he broke off and his cheeks flushed again, she almost laughed more. What stopped her was his sincerity. The last thing she wanted to do was hurt the feelings of a man who had risked his life to help her and was apparently going to continue to do so until ordered to stop. The fact that she thought he'd been about to confess having personal concern for her was doubly sobering.

She reached to touch his sleeve, to comfort him, to demonstrate her own sense of caring. "I apologize for teasing you. I know you take your responsibilities very seriously. I feel the same about mine, which is why it's so hurtful when even my boss thinks I'm capable of the horrible things my supposed twin's been doing." She paused to sniffle. "Can we still go to Montana and look for witnesses there?"

It was a relief when Colt nodded. "Hopefully tomorrow. In the meantime, you're staying with me at the Stark Lodge."

"I beg your pardon?"

"Don't worry. You will have your own room as long as Sampson sleeps next to your bed."

"Let me guess. He snores."

"Like a freight train. But he'll also protect you."

"He's not trained for that, is he?"

"No, but his instincts are good. And I won't be far away."

Another silly response crept into Brooke's thoughts. As much as she yearned to lighten the somber mood, she left it unsaid. After all, with the K-9 cop and his dog close by, her chances of being harmed were lessened. That conclusion should have helped her relax but it had the opposite effect.

Colt and Sampson could have been seriously injured, or worse, during the crash, and the fact that all three of them had walked away unscathed was wonderful. It had been unlikely, yet there they were, fit and fine. Suppose things didn't turn out as well the next time somebody wanted to get to her? Suppose she ended up being responsible for them being hurt? If their theories were valid, two innocent strangers had already paid a debt they hadn't owed because someone was trying to destroy her.

That must not happen again, Brooke vowed. Not to

anybody. Especially not to the sweet bloodhound she'd grown so fond of.

She smiled to herself as she finished the thought silently...and honestly. There was no doubt she was very fond of the K-9 and, truth to tell, her feelings toward his human partner were even stronger, and more tender.

Yes, she knew Colt was only carrying out orders from his chief. She also knew he could be reassigned at a moment's notice. Would that happen? Maybe, maybe not. What truly mattered was that he was there with her now and that he cared. He believed in her innocence and had stood up for her in spite of strong evidence to the contrary.

If Brooke had been asked what made a perfect friend and companion, she could have answered by merely pointing to Colt Maxwell. Something about him spoke to her heart, and her fondest hope at the moment was that she could continue to mask her burgeoning affection and keep her evil twin from guessing how much she cared. Failure to do so could identify Colt as another way to hurt her, to bring her down. She would push him away and deny any romantic inclinations, of course. The problem was, it was already too late to prevent those thoughts from filling her mind and heart.

TWELVE

Colt had arranged for them, and their belongings, to be dropped off at the Stark Lodge, just outside the west border of Mt. Rainier National Park. What he had not counted on was finding the lodge full so early in the season. "Are you sure?" he asked the desk clerk.

"Positive. Sorry, sir."

Colt turned to Brooke. "Okay, you and Sampson can have my room."

"Then where will you sleep?"

That was, unfortunately, a question he had no answer for. "I'll work something out."

"What, sleep in your car? Oops, can't do that. No car. Besides, it still gets too cold at night for that. Forget it. I'm not tossing you out of your room."

There was one thing he could try. "Is Eli Ballard in the lodge today? I'd like to speak with him."

"No, sir. Sorry. Mr. Luke Stark, the co-owner, is here, though. Will he do?" The clerk had a telephone receiver in his hand and was poised to dial.

Knowing that Luke was eventually going to inherit his late sister Stacey's business enterprises, Colt agreed with a nod. Eli and Stacey had been partners in three Stark Lodges, each of them near Washington State National Parks, and it had been over a month since her tragic death. Perhaps her brother could help.

"All right. I'll talk to Luke."

Within five minutes, the tall, dark-haired man with military bearing entered the lobby and approached Colt with his hand outstretched. "Good to see you again, Officer. Is there news about Stacey's murder?"

"Sorry. That's not why I'm here." Colt shook Luke's hand firmly, then turned to indicate Brooke. "Do you know Ranger Stevens?"

"I believe we may have met." He nodded politely toward her.

Colt continued. "There's been some additional trouble in the park and she needs a place to stay, just for tonight." Seeing Luke glance at the desk clerk, Colt added, "All your rooms are booked."

"I see." Luke shrugged. "Well, I could recommend one of our competitors, like the Ashford Inn and Suites, but we're not exactly on the best of terms with Oliver Roscoe and Lynda Mack, or with most of our other rivals, as you may know. Eli Ballard even wonders if one of them might have been behind the murders."

"I'd heard about that and know our team has been following up," Colt replied.

Apparently getting an idea, Luke smiled and palmed his cell phone, spoke briefly, then smiled at Brooke. "Danica Hayes, one of Colt's colleagues in the PNK9 Unit, has offered to share the room we made available to her while she's assigned to the Stark-Digby murder case. She was going to watch my baby son for me this evening, but it turns out I'm off from the hospital tonight so I'll keep Caden with me." Colt knew that Luke, a former army medic, had come home from overseas when he'd become the sole parent of his son.

"That's a relief to hear. What Colt didn't tell you is that I'm the target of a stalker. I certainly wouldn't want to endanger anyone else, especially not a child."

Luke nodded in understanding. "Danica's room is the safest in the whole state. She's a cop and bunks with an attack-trained German shepherd."

"Oh! I know who you mean. I heard you might be serious about *her*." Brooke acted thrilled, and Colt didn't doubt her sincerity. She was practically jumping up and down with joy. "I love her dog. Hutch, right?"

"Yes, that's him." Luke was blushing as he spoke into his phone again, then looked up. "She says yes. I'll have more towels sent to the room. Anything else you need?"

Apparently Danica had assured him she was well prepared so he turned back to Colt and Brooke. "It's all settled. She's been helping me get used to taking care of a baby. It's been quite an adjustment, but with Danica in my life things are working out."

"My condolences about your sister," Brooke said, "and thank you for helping. My story is long and complicated. Colt can fill you in if it's not against the rules. Personally, all I worry about is being mistaken for somebody else and blamed again."

Luke looked puzzled. "Blamed?"

Making a face, Brooke explained, "Yeah. If all they were considering was DNA evidence, I'd be on trial for multiple murders." She studied the dark-haired man's face. "Is it still okay for me to bunk with Danica?"

Answering for Luke, Colt said, "I trust Brooke with my life," and realized how true that statement was. He did trust her. Implicitly. When Luke gestured toward the small restaurant inside the inn and said, "Let's go have a cup of coffee and talk," Colt was more than ready to oblige. Brooke hung back.

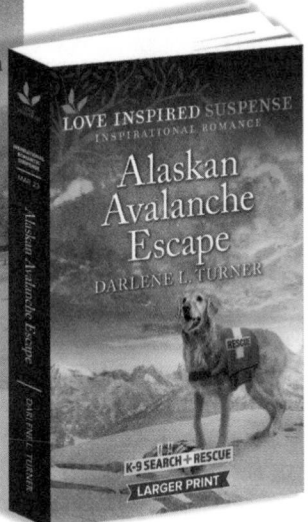

LOYAL READER
FREE BOOKS VOUCHER

BUSINESS REPLY MAIL
FIRST-CLASS MAIL   PERMIT NO. 717   BUFFALO, NY

POSTAGE WILL BE PAID BY ADDRESSEE

HARLEQUIN READER SERVICE
PO BOX 1341
BUFFALO NY 14240-8571

NO POSTAGE
NECESSARY
IF MAILED
IN THE
UNITED STATES

"Aren't you joining us?" Colt asked her.

"If you don't mind, I'd rather sit here by the fire. I'm suddenly exhausted."

"Considering the morning we've had I'm not surprised." He eyed the archway to the coffee bar, then offered her Sampson's leash. "You keep the K-9. I'll sit where I can keep an eye on both of you."

Luke paused and tilted his head quizzically. "You had a rough morning?"

"Oh, yeah," Colt said. "C'mon. I should be able to fill you in by the time we've finished eight or ten cups."

"That bad?" Luke's right eyebrow lifted to punctuate the question.

Before Colt could answer, he heard Brooke call after them. "Worse."

Brooke had propped up her feet and nearly dozed off in one of the chairs arranged to face an enormous hearth. Sampson was using her legs as a makeshift roof by wiggling between the chair and footstool. She didn't have to look to know Colt was keeping his promise to watch her. Not that he needed to worry with his big dog on duty. The bloodhound might resemble a child's plush, floppy-eared toy when he was resting, but she'd seen him in action. When he wanted to, Brooke knew Sampson could be as formidable as Hutch was—he just didn't seem to want to very often. That was fine with her. Being with the laid-back K-9 was more relaxing than trying to keep up appearances for her human guard.

She sighed and sank down in the plush chair. Warm fire, comfy chair, occasionally snoring dog and gentle, semiclassical music playing in the background combined to lull her until she closed her eyes and let herself drift in and out of light sleep.

Brooke rarely recalled her dreams although they did sometimes awaken her in a fright. This time, she heard a disembodied voice saying "Murderer" as plainly as if someone was whispering it in her ear.

She stirred. Moaned. Crossed her arms and slid another inch lower. Something bumped her chair. Jostled the footstool. Blinking awake, she thought she sensed a malevolent presence, although she couldn't pinpoint its source.

Sampson stood, knocking into her legs and dropping her deeper into the easy chair. Unbalanced, she struggled to get her feet on the floor and keep from sliding all the way down. She'd never heard the K-9 growl before, but there was no doubt something was bothering him right now.

As soon as Sampson gave her enough space to maneuver, she turned onto her side, put her palms on the seat of the chair and pushed off her knees.

Sampson began to bark with an urgency and seriousness that caused everyone in the lobby to freeze and stare. Embarrassed to have caused such a ruckus, Brooke was about to give his leash a tug when she heard a familiar voice.

Across the lobby, Colt was on his feet, waving his arms, and shouted, "Stop. Brooke, stop."

For an instant she thought he was telling her to stop correcting his K-9. Then she realized he wasn't looking at her at all. His gaze was fixed on a woman with reddish hair who was literally running out the front door.

Her jaw gaped. Breathing in gasps, she managed to say his name. "Colt?" A second try produced enough sound to capture his attention in spite of the noisy dog. "Colt!"

His head swiveled from the woman going out the door to the place where Brooke was now standing with Sampson. The bloodhound was sounding off with howls loud enough to almost shake the windows.

Brooke could hardly believe her eyes. *Was that...?* It had

to be. Which meant she had been close enough to Brooke to harm her despite the dog at her feet and a law officer positioned to see everything. Had Sampson's growls stopped whatever her twin had planned? It was highly likely. And she was truly, truly grateful.

Colt had already taken several strides toward the door when Brooke had shouted his name. He skidded to a stop, did a double take, then changed direction and ran to her.

She stepped into his arms as if they always greeted each other that way, put her cheek on his chest and shuddered. "Was that her again?"

"I didn't see her face. When I saw that red hair I thought for a second you were leaving after you'd promised to stay put. I was planning to stop you."

"I wish you had. Maybe all this would be over if you'd grabbed her."

"Not and leave you," he countered. "Even if that was her, we can't be certain she's working alone."

Brooke held tightly to him. "I'd never thought of that."

"Anything is possible. We have to stay on alert all the time. It's my fault. I never should have left you."

"Sampson was on the job," Brooke assured him. "I was half-asleep but I think it was his growling that scared her off." Scowling, she leaned away to look up at Colt. "I think she said something to me but everything's sort of foggy. I can't remember what it was."

"Maybe you'll think of it later."

"Aren't you going to report the sighting?"

"Luke is doing that for us." He reached down to pat Sampson on the head. "I'd use him to try to track her if it didn't mean leaving you alone."

"Then take me to Danica's room. I'll be fine with her and Hutch."

Colt spoke to his K-9 as if it understood. "Hear that?

She's trying to get rid of us, and after all the effort you put into telling me something was wrong."

"I am grateful. To both of you," Brooke said, going along with the joke. "But I suspect the lodge visitors would prefer a little less baying and a little more elevator music."

"I'll have you know Sampson has perfect pitch. He was singing harmony beautifully."

"Is that so?" Brooke had to laugh in spite of her recent scare. Suddenly, she sobered. "I remember."

Colt still had one arm around her shoulders, lending moral support. "What? Is it a clue?"

"No." Tears filled Brooke's eyes as she slowly shook her head. "No. All I heard her say was *murderer.*"

"Then it had to be your twin. Only she would know for sure you're being framed."

"Alleged twin," Brooke said. "We haven't proved anything yet."

"We will. I know it and so do you, so why the hesitancy?"

Sighing audibly, she searched her mind for answers that made sense. Some did, some didn't. And some were too personal to share, particularly with this empathetic cop who had already found a place in her heart.

"I guess I don't want to believe it," Brooke began. "I've spent my whole life thinking I was an only child. It's hard to accept having a sibling, let alone a twin."

"You know she exists. You've seen her. We both have."

"Probably." The stern expression on Colt's face caused her to concede. "Okay. Yes. I know there is a woman my age who resembles me and whose DNA can be mistaken for mine. Satisfied?"

"Sure. If you don't want to use the term *twin*, we won't. Have you figured out why that bothers you so much?"

She had but she wasn't about to explain it to him. The

existence of someone so closely related yet so different—
so wrong—tainted her. It wasn't as if she could simply dis-
own a family member whose actions were embarrassing.
An identical twin was more closely attached. Impossible
to deny. And that meant that she, Brooke, carried the same
traits, the same DNA, the same blood as a stone-cold killer.

THIRTEEN

Once Brooke was safely secured with Danica, Colt returned to the lobby and tried to set Sampson on the trail of the woman he'd seen fleeing the lodge. Instead of striking a trail right away, however, the K-9 seemed confused and kept trying to follow the scent trail he knew Brooke had left when he'd escorted her upstairs.

"Well, at least you defended her when she needed you," Colt told the dog. "That's something."

Sampson's tail was wagging but the droop of his long ears and the sagging skin around his eyes and jowls gave him a woeful expression. Colt felt the way his K-9 looked. He'd made a mistake by not chasing down the suspect when he had the chance and the real reason for making that error was personal. That made it worse. Much worse. He had failed at his assignment by putting Brooke ahead of catching a killer and that choice was inexcusable.

Pausing on a bench near the lodge, he called his boss. Confession was necessary whether he liked it or not. Part of him hoped he'd be understood and forgiven while another part wondered if the chief would decide to replace him on the Stevens case and whether it would be wise to argue against it.

Before he'd decided, Donovan answered. "Colt. No aftereffects from the accident?"

"None."

"Sampson okay, too? The ranger?"

"They're both fine. So am I, except for my pride."

Donovan chuckled. "Goes with the job. Let yourself get too proud of your special classification and something or someone is bound to come along and knock you off your pedestal. What happened? Was it the accident?"

"No, no. There's concrete proof we were attacked and shoved off the road by a heavier vehicle. Nobody could have withstood that unless they'd outrun the assailant, and fog prevented that."

"Then what?"

"I had the chance to nab the person we think is the killer, and I let her get away."

"Whoa. Explain."

"She looked enough like Brooke to confuse me. I mistook her for Brooke until I saw the real one and chose to return to her, instead of continuing in pursuit of the fake."

"Spur-of-the-moment decision, right?"

"Yes, but..."

"We all make them every day. Some are better than others. What influenced your choice?"

Colt cleared his throat, then plunged ahead. "That's what I'm trying to tell you. At the time I was sure, but in retrospect, it wasn't rational. I could see that Brooke was okay but I turned away from the suspect and went to her instead."

"You chose Stevens."

"Yes. I should have kept after the other woman. Because I didn't, she managed to disappear again and she's out there, probably plotting her next attack."

"At least we know she's still in the area. Do you think she'll go back into the park?"

"She will if Brooke Stevens does. In the meantime, I'm

at a disadvantage because I'm on foot and Brooke is still in danger. I know she is."

"You'll get no argument from me on that," Donovan said. "Is she still willing to fly to Montana with you?"

"I'm sure she is," Colt replied. "She isn't keen on flying but driving is out of the question, especially now."

"Takes too long, anyway." Colt could hear papers being shuffled. "Catch a ride with one of the rangers from Mount Rainier and report to the Ashford High School athletic field at dawn tomorrow," Fanelli said. "A chopper will pick you up and bring you to headquarters before taking you to Montana."

"I'd planned to leave Sampson there for a health checkup, anyway. Will that work out?"

"I'll see he has an appointment for a complete physical."

"Thanks."

"And, Colt…" His pause made Colt listen intently. "The next time you have a tough choice to make, rely on instinct the way you did today. Don't waste time doubting yourself. I know your heart is right about this job. Follow it."

"Thanks for the vote of confidence. I'm going to give Sampson another hour to search, then quit. We're not making much progress."

"Your decision. See you tomorrow."

Colt ended the call and pocketed his phone. Although he'd wanted to argue about Donovan's conclusion, he was glad he'd held his peace. Perhaps his heart, rather than being 100 percent cop, was what had led him astray this time. It was certainly possible. The last thing he wanted to do was ruin his reputation or that of the PNK9 Unit by making foolish errors.

Taking that one step further, he suddenly realized that he and Brooke were more connected than he'd originally thought. Innocents were being killed, like his own mother had been, and the one responsible was closely related to her, just as his cruel father had been to him. They shared the genetic propensity for evil the same way people inherited blue eyes or dark red hair and freckles.

No wonder he'd felt such a kinship with her. No matter what they did or how honestly, how perfectly, they lived their lives, they would always remember their tainted origins. Always carry the burden of knowing about the terrible deeds of someone close to them. The hard truth was inescapable.

Groaning when she woke up the next morning, Brooke stretched and realized how sore the plunge off the road had left her. A two-inch-wide bruise started on her right shoulder and ran across her sternum, not to mention the aches in her legs and arms, probably from the strain of climbing out of the SUV and dodging bullets.

Since Danica had already left with Hutch, Brooke grabbed her traveling bag, made sure the door locked behind her and led Sampson downstairs. A fresh pot of coffee and Colt were waiting. He handed her a steaming foam cup and took the leash. "Drink up while I walk the dog. Our ride will be here in five."

"Cream and sugar?"

"Picky, picky, picky," he teased. "Next thing I know you'll want another egg-and-bacon sandwich like yesterday."

"I only got one bite of that one thanks to your trick and fancy driving," Brooke countered, smiling. "Good thing Danica fed me last night or I'd be skin and bones."

The corners of his blue eyes crinkled in a smile as Colt blushed. "You look about right to me."

Laughing, she watched him lead his K-9 partner out the door. There was something liberating about wearing civilian clothes, although she also missed the ease of donning a uniform. A few friends had teased her about choosing to join the forest service because the green color complemented her hair and hazel eyes, but she knew otherwise. She'd picked a career that had to do with the preservation of nature partly out of guilt for what her father's oil business was doing to the environment. In retrospect, she realized that her biggest mistake had been in telling him about it.

What about her birth parents? she wondered. What were they like? Until she'd started having trouble with this unknown twin of hers it had been easier to imagine her original mom and dad as sweet, naive teens who had sought the best life for an unexpected baby. Now, Brooke didn't know what to think.

Cautiously sipping her hot coffee with both hands, she cradled the cup and watched Colt and Sampson. They had crossed the road into a wooded area and were passing behind a stand of pines... Douglas fir, she corrected, the same way she would if she was leading one of her nature walks for a group of tourists. Soon, the days would warm enough to bring forth the wildflowers in the alpine meadows and her days would be filled with everyone admiring their beauty. When winter blanketed those open areas it was hard to imagine the pristine loveliness that hid beneath the ice and snow, yet when summer came, there were the drifts of colorful flowers, just as there had been before every year. Cycles were predictable. Spring promised summer, and summer led to fall, when the wilderness slowed down and prepared for its long sleep. And then came rejuvenation.

It was people who couldn't be predicted, Brooke decided with a sigh. They were the problem. Always had been. That was the rub. That was why she felt so uneasy.

Not only were others hard to figure out, but she also wasn't doing a good job of understanding herself.

What made her who she was? Jo and B. J. Stevens got some of the credit, of course. They had loved and nurtured her the same way she and her fellow rangers tried to protect the national parks from the ravages of too many tourists. If she hadn't been so well cared for, what might she have become? Could she have gone wrong, too? Or if her parents had adopted both baby girls, would she have a sister to love who was like herself?

Lost in a sea of unanswerable questions, Brooke gazed out at the woods across from the lodge entrance. Colt and Sampson had been visible a second ago. Where were they now?

She set aside her coffee cup, zipped her jacket and pushed open the front door to get a wider view from the porch. Cold wind ruffled her long hair and bit through the fabric of her jeans. She pulled on a hat with earflaps, then gloves. There was a lot to be said for the forest-green ranger uniform if a person wanted to keep warm in icy weather.

Squinting against unfiltered sunlight shining through the trees to the east, she shaded her eyes with one hand and peered into the distance. That was when she heard it. The sound of a bloodhound, baying.

The only way to handle her cell phone properly was barehanded, so she pulled off the gloves, found the number Colt had given her and called it.

He didn't answer. The call went to voice mail. She ended it and tried again. Still nothing.

Wheeling around, she stuck her head inside, looking for aid. There was no one on the front desk and no sign of any other residents. If she'd thought to take down Danica's number she'd have called her, but she hadn't even considered needing it.

The only other numbers she had were for her ranger station, Georgia Henning's cell and assorted fast-food establishments in and around Ashford. Instead, she dialed 911.

"Nine-one-one, what's your emergency?"

"This is Park Ranger Brooke Stevens. I'm at the Stark Lodge near Ashford. K-9 Officer Colt Maxwell and his dog have gone into the woods across from the lodge and he's not answering his phone. His dog is baying. I need you to contact the PNK9 Unit and get him some help."

The dispatcher failed to match Brooke's concern. "I understand your concern, but if there's no crime to report I'm afraid we can't. You'll need to contact the other agency yourself."

"But…"

"I'm sorry. If you have a true emergency, please call us back."

Dumbfounded, Brooke stared at her cell phone. Hearing Sampson howling might not be a scary sign to most people, but it sure concerned her.

She knew, without a doubt, that she should stay right where she was and wait for Colt to return. And she did try. For at least three minutes, maybe four.

Then she took one step off the curb. And another, and another, until she had crossed the roadway and stood on the opposite side.

She muttered, "Go back," and knew that was exactly what she should do, but she ignored her sensible instincts and started off in the direction of the troubling animal sounds.

Sampson had struck a trail almost as soon as they'd left the road, and Colt had allowed it because the dog was never wrong. Whatever or whoever he was after, it mattered. Of all the K-9s Colt had worked with, this one was his favorite. Granted, most trainers and handlers were biased. That was to be expected. But in Sampson's case all the praise was warranted.

Colt's phone rang. He ignored it in favor of paying attention and staying on his feet while Sampson dragged him in and out of gullies, over boulders and between close-set trees. The third time the phone rang, he pulled it out to check the caller. Seeing a name was enough to make him rein in the dog and answer. "Brooke! What's wrong."

"You are. Where are you? You disappeared and I could hear Sampson howling."

"He struck a trail. Wait for me. I'll be back soon."

The K-9 strained at the end of his lead. That pulled Colt sideways into a tree and he bounced off. The cell phone landed in wet leaves. By the time he picked it up, Brooke's voice sounded panicky, so he reassured her. "I'm okay, I'm okay."

As she replied, it took him a few seconds to realize what she was saying. "You did what?"

"I—I was worried about you and the police refused to take me seriously so I came out to see for myself."

Colt was livid. "You left the lodge? After all we've been through and everything that's happened, you just walked out? Unbelievable."

"I know, I know. It was dumb," she grumbled. "But I didn't go very far. I was worried, okay? You could have answered your phone the first time I called."

"I was busy working the dog. He picked up a trail and I assumed he was remembering scents from before."

"They can do that? Remember, I mean?"

"Sampson can." Fighting to control a temper heightened by worry, he asked, "Do you have a clue where you are?"

"Yes. Of course. It's a straight shot back to the lodge."

"Okay. I'm pulling him off this trail and coming to you."

"No. Let him go on. I'm fine. I'm…" She broke off.

"Brooke?" He shouted into the phone. "Brooke!"

"Shush. I heard something. It was probably a squirrel."

"Or a bear," Colt countered.

"Look, I need to put the phone down so I can pick up a branch big enough for self-defense. Okay? Then I'll head straight for the lodge. Meet you there."

Colt intended to order her to leave the line open and stay connected. Before he had a chance to speak, however, she had apparently done exactly that because he could still hear muffled sounds, as if the phone was now in her pocket. Wood cracked. Boots stomped on brittle twigs. Then she began to breathe harder.

She was on the move. Headed back to the inn, as promised. At least something was going right this morning. Disgusted, Colt called Sampson to heel and doubled back. The sounds of his and Sampson's breathing drowned out sounds coming from Brooke unless he stopped, held very still and put the phone to his ear, so he did that periodically.

A strange noise outside caused him to stop again and listen for her.

This time, there was the unmistakable high pitch of a woman's scream.

FOURTEEN

Holding her breath, Brooke had not intended to make any noise. She was gripping a fallen tree branch with both hands, like a baseball bat, waiting for someone or something to appear.

An almost whispered "hello" from directly behind her was so startling, she momentarily lost control and screamed.

The face she saw when she whirled was such a shock that the branch fell from her grip. It was her—only it clearly wasn't. This face was hard, the hazel eyes glittering with perceived hate, the auburn hair flyaway and tangled.

Brooke was speechless. Nothing she'd imagined was as traumatic as this meeting. It was more than seeing a mirror image of herself. It was as if she could glimpse a hidden facet of her own personality that she'd never seen before.

Unable to make her feet move or her lips form words, Brooke reached out with one hand, needing a solid touch as proof.

The other woman jerked back, as if she'd received an electric shock, retreating one step, then another. She halted when she and Brooke were a dozen feet apart. Other than her initial *hello*, she'd said nothing else.

"Please?" Brooke asked, barely a whisper and almost a prayer.

That one word broke the mental connection. Instead of attacking when she could have, the other woman spun around and began to run, zigzagging past large trees and plowing through the undergrowth. In seconds, she'd disappeared.

Tears filled Brooke's eyes and began to trickle down her cheeks. Her initial fear was systematically replaced with surprising empathy for the frightened woman. She reached a trembling hand into her pocket to retrieve her cell phone. It showed the call to Colt still active.

"I'm—I'm okay," Brooke told him.

"Where are you?"

"Almost back to the lodge."

"Was that you I heard scream?"

Nodding as if he could see her, she said, "Probably."

"Why? Are you in danger?"

"No." Her breath shuddered, as if she was chilled to the bone.

"Okay. Sampson and I are on the way."

"She—she was here," Brooke spluttered. "I saw her. Right in front of me."

"Your twin?"

She could tell Colt was running because he was breathing like a marathon runner. "Yes." Pausing, she frowned, lowered the phone and listened to her surroundings. "Colt?"

"Yeah?"

"I hear something. It can't be her. She ran the other direction. Somebody else is out here, too."

Sampson had the lead and Colt kept up with him. Barely. On a smooth track, no man could have kept pace with the athletically fit dog, but with its nose to the ground and moving back and forth looking for a scent trail, Sampson was making slower forward progress.

They mounted a rise and there she was. Safe and sound in the same clothing she'd been wearing. His already racing heart leaped and gave wings to his feet. "Brooke!"

She turned her head a little but didn't respond the way he'd expected.

"Brooke?"

Something moved in the distance. A figure was making its way through the woods and heading straight for her. Colt shouted into the phone. "Brooke, answer me. Who is that?" He looked at the screen. Their connection was gone.

Colt tripped, kept hold of his phone and broke his fall with the other hand—the hand that had been holding Sampson's leash. The eager bloodhound was off like a shot, aimed straight for Brooke.

Staggering to his feet, Colt followed, praying silently that he would be in time to save both his dog and the ranger whose well-being was in his hands.

He still had twenty or thirty yards to go when he saw Sampson join Brooke and wiggle at her feet like a happy puppy, rather than a protector or an attacking K-9. She grabbed the loose leash and began to coil the extra length.

Arriving breathless, Colt put up a hand to catch himself and slapped the tree near where she was standing. Now that he was in position to see who had her attention, he greeted the lodge owner. "Hello, Eli. I asked to see you last night. Your desk clerk referred me to Luke Stark instead."

The dark-haired man smiled. "Yes—Luke. That's fine. But I do hate to burden him with lodge business when he hasn't decided if he's going to keep his sister's share."

"He was very helpful," Colt said, still fighting to catch his breath.

Eli nodded. "We've arranged for him to keep his suite at the lodge. Your colleague, who is helping him with his little boy, is temporarily using Stacey's old room. I thought that was the least I could do."

"So he told us," Colt said, not as impressed by the supposedly magnanimous gesture as he figured Eli had intended. Eli Ballard wasn't a suspect; he had an alibi for the double homicide and barely a motive since the lodges were in financial trouble, but no one closely linked to murder victims could be discounted entirely. "What brought you so far from comfort this early?"

The man straightened his tailored coat. "Just taking a walk to clear my head. It's been…hard. It helps to commune with nature from time to time."

Colt nodded and slipped an arm around Brooke's shoulders, then pulled her closer, taking control of Sampson's leash at the same time. "Nice seeing you."

Beside him, he felt Brooke leaning in and sensed her relief. That made two of them. The sooner he could get her away from Mt. Rainier and into the air, where she wouldn't be so vulnerable, the better he'd like it.

From behind, Eli said, "A pleasure," as they walked away together.

Colt made sure they were out of earshot before he bent and asked quietly, "Where did he come from?"

"The lodge, I guess."

"Did he show up right after your twin left you?"

"It wasn't long." Brooke was frowning. "When I saw her I just stood there like a department-store mannequin. I didn't even try to reason with her. I'm sorry."

"I don't know what I'd have done in your place," Colt said. "It had to be a shock to be face-to-face, even though we'd seen her from a distance."

"It was weird. Really, really strange. As if my brain shut down."

"How did she act? Was she menacing? Were you afraid?"

"Kind of," Brooke replied as they crossed the parking lot and approached the rustic inn. "I don't honestly know what I felt at the time."

Colt gave her shoulders a supportive squeeze. "Give yourself time. You can mull it over on the flight."

"We're still going?"

"Yes. Getting you out of her reach, even for a day, will give us both time to decompress."

"I can tell you one thing," Brooke said pensively.

Waiting, Colt met her gaze and noticed new tears behind her long lashes.

"She wasn't like me on the inside. I don't know how I know, I just do. Meeting her was like encountering a stranger who gives off bad vibes. Know what I mean?"

"I do," Colt said. "I used to question the validity of that gift, but I don't anymore. Sometimes we just know, in our hearts, when something is right or wrong."

"Yes."

This was the moment when he could continue with praise of her as a person and suggest that they had grown close so quickly because of that kind of spiritual connection. However, he did not. Nor was he planning to in the future. Brooke's life was already complicated to the breaking point. He wasn't going to add to her angst by inferring they might be soul mates. Even if they actually were, which he strongly suspected, that didn't mean it was wise to pursue the notion.

Colt sighed, resigned to suffering in silence. He was the son of a convicted murderer. No matter what Brooke eventually learned about her twin, his history was guaranteed to turn her stomach. Why not? It turned his every time he was foolish enough to allow himself to remember.

* * *

Listening to Colt reporting the sighting of the suspect near the Stark Lodge, Brooke let her mind wander. When bits and pieces of the encounter came back to her out of order, she accepted them. Psychologists claimed that the human brain would fill in blanks in memory if the truth wasn't readily available and she wanted to recall as many facts as possible before that happened to her.

The trek in the woods had made them late for their appointment with the helicopter. Fortunately, the pilot had been informed of the delay and had waited.

Brooke wasn't too nervous until she saw how small the white, yellow and black chopper was up close. She'd seen them called in for rescue before, but had never had to actually climb into one. "Oh, dear."

Thanking the park ranger who had driven them from the lodge, Colt retrieved Sampson and their meager luggage. Their planned one-day trip was already into its second day, but unless they got caught in a spring storm or otherwise delayed, they should have packed enough of everything.

A portable crate for Sampson was secured next to the cramped rear seat in the chopper. Colt and the pilot helped Brooke climb in next to it and showed her how to fasten the shoulder harness. This was it, she mused. The moment of truth. Her last chance to refuse to fly.

Well, that wasn't going to happen. She wanted to go to Hungry Horse and seek out the staff of the defunct adoption agency and if she had to sit in a little metal bucket hanging from flimsy-looking rotors like the propellers on a kid's beanie and risk her life to do it, she would. Somebody knew the truth about her birth and adoption and she was going to locate them if it was the last thing she did.

Thanks to the noise of the engine and beating of the blades against the air, Brooke was the only one who heard herself when she said, "Bad, bad choice of words," then almost chuckled.

What was most confusing was why her doppelgänger hadn't harmed her when they'd been face-to-face, both in the hotel lobby and in the woods.

Brooke sighed. Colt had hinted that everybody in his unit was assuming the motive was a personal vendetta, but if that was true, what was the aim? Two hikers had died, both killed with the gun stolen from her cabin, and by impersonating her, her reputation was being damaged, too. Was that what her twin wanted? Was the destruction supposed to be emotional rather than physical? If that was true, then why push Colt's SUV off the road? Why shoot at it on the side road and down in the canyon? Nothing made sense.

Assessing the situation helped take her mind off the flight and keep her from obsessing about the sensation she was hanging by the string of a helium balloon and being dragged through the sky with no safety net. Although she did flinch several times when the pilot banked to show his passengers interesting terrain below, she managed to keep from squealing. Well, except for once or twice when she'd felt the restraints tighten to hold her in her seat.

At her feet, cozy in his portable kennel, Sampson closed his eyes and went to sleep. That actually helped Brooke relax. Of course, this was her first chopper ride and the trained K-9 had probably traveled this way more than once. Nevertheless, she was glad for Sampson's company because Colt and the pilot were talking to each other via radio headsets and there was no chance she'd be able to communicate with either of them unless she had one, too.

Finally, she tapped Colt on the shoulder, and he turned to look at her. She thought she saw his lips form a sentence asking if she was okay. Instead of assuming she was right, she cupped a hand around her ear and leaned as far forward as the harness would let her, then shouted, "What?"

It didn't take him long to figure out what she wanted and hand her a spare headset, then show her where to plug it in. Except for being larger and more secure, it wasn't very different from listening to music through earbuds.

Grinning, she gave him a thumbs-up sign. "Can you hear me?"

"Loud and clear," Colt said.

"So what did you two have to discuss that you didn't want me to know about?" she asked.

The two men looked at each other for a moment before Colt answered. "We weren't trying to keep anything from you. I just thought it would be best if you rested while you could."

"Uh-huh."

"It's the truth," Colt said.

It was hard to tell voice inflection through the radio because of background noise and static. "I want to believe you. Really I do. How about a quick recap?"

"Sure. The weather is good in Montana. We're going to be stopping in Olympia soon to off-load Sampson and if there's time I'll give you a quick tour of our unit."

"I'd rather get to Hungry Horse and get the search over as soon as possible," Brooke said, hoping he'd agree. "Can't I see your headquarters on the way back?"

It was a short reach to wiggle her fingers through the barred door of the kennel box, and when Sampson roused himself to lick them, it made her smile. She dearly loved this goofy-looking hero with four paws and enormous, velvety ears that hung down farther than the tip of his nose, and it seemed the feeling was mutual.

Loving the dog was the easy part. How she was starting to feel about his human partner was a lot more confusing.

She'd left the security of the lodge and ostensibly risked her life at the mere thought Colt might be in danger. That kind of reaction wasn't rational under any circumstances and she was still berating herself for doing it.

But neither was what had happened when she'd come face-to-face with a mirror image of herself. Brooke sighed and settled back as the helicopter circled a marked area on the ground, preparing to land. Maybe *she* was the problem. Ever since the hiker had been found murdered on one of her trails, she'd been jumpy, and when Sampson had turned up a second body behind her cabin, she'd been flabbergasted. Had learning about the matching DNA pushed her over the edge? Unhinged her? Was she jumping at shadows because she was as unbalanced as her twin seemed to be? Those tendencies could be genetic, she knew, even if they never actually manifested themselves.

The chopper touched down as gently as a slipper on a plush rug. Colt waited for the blades to slow, then ducked out his side and reached in to free his K-9. "They're waiting for me," he told Brooke. "Sit tight. I'll be right back."

Not like she had a lot of choice, she thought. The pilot remained, too. He removed his headset, so she took hers off and tapped him on the shoulder. "Was Colt telling the truth? About your conversation, I mean."

What she had expected was confirmation or a flat refusal to discuss what had been talked about. Instead, he smiled and said, "Mostly."

"Mostly? What wasn't true?"

"The part about good weather around Kalispell," he said with a smile. "Might get a little rough."

"Rough, like waves on a lake, or rough like a tsunami?"

The pilot shrugged. The brim of his cap shadowed his forehead but she still saw one eyebrow arch. "Probably something in between. But don't worry. I've flown in worse."

"Well, *I* haven't."

Chuckling, he reached into a side pocket on the console and handed her a paper bag.

Brooke was not amused.

FIFTEEN

When Colt returned to the chopper, he glanced at Brooke. Instead of the smile he expected, she made a face at him.

"What did you do to her while I was gone?" he asked the pilot.

Flipping switches and revving up the engine, he said, "Nothing."

Brooke replaced her headset as Colt donned his and chimed in, "Ha! You lied to me about the bad weather."

"I did not." Colt made a fist and playfully slugged the pilot on his right bicep. "Thanks, buddy."

"Just trying to keep the passengers entertained."

"By scaring me to death?" Brooke asked. In spite of being the brunt of the joke, Colt was pleased by how well she took it when she added, "Just you wait. You'll get yours."

Although he was laughing along with her and the pilot, Colt silently hoped she'd still be in a position to joke with her fellow rangers and support staff in the future.

Her goal was to confirm that she really had a twin, though that wasn't really in doubt, and to find out all she could about the woman.

His goal was different. He was there to support Brooke Stevens and prove she was innocent, and the only way to do that was to prove someone else had committed the crimes. Someone who might come to mean something to her in the future. After all, she and the unnamed twin were siblings. Whether or not they had known about each other before, they did now, and Colt was fairly certain that Brooke would come to feel a connection to her sister, particularly once they'd met officially. Kinship mattered. People might convince themselves that they didn't care about relatives who were different from the norm, but deep down, where it counted, they had to.

Sadly, he was no different in regard to his late father, Colt admitted. There was a part of that man he hated, yet faith insisted he forgive. Talk about hard to do. He'd been working on that since his teens and was still struggling. Perhaps he always would. It was one thing to know how important it was to not carry a grudge and quite another to actually let go of the memories that kept it alive.

If it had been safe to do so, Colt would have moved to the rear seat next to Brooke, so he could see her expression as he tried to explain his conclusions with regard to her birth family. To prove empathy, he'd have to tell her about his own family and that was information few people were privy to outside his closest circle of friends. Donovan knew. So did Asher Gilmore because Colt had thought the story might help Asher deal with his shaky relationship to his half sister, Mara. They'd just been starting to get to know each other, as colleagues and siblings, when Mara had fled from the scene of the double murder.

Brooke's voice over the com link broke into Colt's thoughts and made him smile. "Are we there yet?"

"Almost," Colt said over his shoulder. "If you're getting bored, look below. That's Glacier National Park to the east and the Rocky Mountains."

"Beautiful." Her voice carried true appreciation of what they were seeing.

The first thing that popped into Colt's mind when he heard the word *beautiful* was not the awesome scenery below, it was the ranger seated behind him. His opinion included her heart as well as her outward appearance. That was the key. And that was the difference between her and her twin. The hair, the eyes, even the smattering of freckles might be the same, but the essence of what made each of them special was not.

For that difference, Colt was thankful, and he prayed Brooke would also come to that conclusion. If she identified too closely with her twin, that woman's eventual arrest and conviction could be very hard to accept.

If Brooke wasn't the killer, then her twin *was*.

Was he thinking too far ahead? Condemning someone who should be considered innocent until proven guilty? Probably. Definitely, he concluded. That wasn't usually a failing of his, so why do it now?

Because I must prove Brooke is innocent, he told himself. *Right now, she looks so guilty it's scary.*

Expecting a rural village, Brooke was surprised at her first view of Hungry Horse. It was a modern, if small, city with cozy neighborhoods and shopping centers and schools.

She laughed to herself. "Wow, paved roads and everything. When I heard the name of this place I pictured a few shacks in the middle of nowhere."

The chopper landed next to what she assumed was a hospital, since the pad was a bright red circle with a white *X* painted in the center.

Colt helped her down while the pilot off-loaded their overnight bags. Enough wind was still coming from the rotating blades to blow her hair into her eyes, so she grabbed and held it at the nape of her neck until she and Colt had walked away.

"Will he wait for us?" she asked.

"Not there. He's going to refuel in Kalispell and stand by."

"Good. This may take longer than I'd anticipated." She gestured at the neatly groomed lawns and homes across the street from the medical facility. "I'd pictured a town where everything was within walking distance. We may need to rent a car."

"My chief thought of that." Colt checked the map on his phone. "There's a hotel three blocks that way. A car is waiting for us."

"Gotta love those federal perks," Brooke teased.

"Actually, our unit is funded by a grant, but it is administered by the government. That gives us more leeway than the park service has. We can spend money as needed."

"Still, you don't have your own helicopter."

"We don't throw our funds away. If we used one every day the way the National Park Service does, we could justify the added expense."

"Very sensible of you. I suppose the same goes for having separate training facilities in all three parks you cover."

"Right. Olympia is our headquarters, so training is done there, except for field work in each park to familiarize the dogs with various terrain and challenge their brains."

"Sampson is sweet," she said, guessing what Colt's reaction would be. She was right. He smiled like a proud papa.

Brooke had been looking around as they walked. Hungry Horse looked less like winter and more like spring than Mt. Rainier National Park did, with the exception of the lowest elevations. Seeing daffodils already in bloom and tulip leaves spreading wide gave her spirits a lift. "I love spring," she said quietly. "It always reminds me of new beginnings."

"I've been wanting to talk to you about that," Colt said.

She could tell from his tone of voice and body language that things were about to get serious. "Okay. Why?"

"Because as I've gotten to know you, I can see how tenderhearted you are. Remember, this person we're trying to identify is likely not a bit like you. Don't make the mistake of thinking otherwise."

Brooke scowled at him. "I told you I could tell she wasn't."

"I know, I know. You also said it made you feel odd seeing yourself in her. What I'm trying to say is, remember to look beneath the surface. Some people are able to fool observers by changing personalities. Look at how she behaved with that family of park visitors. She's not you. Not even close."

"Thanks, I think. Were you a psych major in college or something?"

"No. I learned it growing up."

Because he hesitated, she waited without probing. This conversation seemed hard for him, and she didn't want to end it by asking too many direct questions.

Finally, Colt went on. "To the outside world, to their friends and fellow church members, my parents looked like the ideal couple. I knew better. I heard quarreling all the time and when Dad started hitting my mother I tried to stop him."

Empathetic, Brooke gently touched his forearm. "I'm sorry."

"He never was. Sorry, I mean. Then one day I came home from school and my mother was missing. Dad said she'd left us. I didn't believe him, but what could I do? The only way to prove he was lying was to locate her and I did try. No computer searches turned her up, so I started to ask friends and neighbors. School counselors got involved when my grades slipped."

Again, he paused. Brooke could tell by the occasional, slight break in his voice that this story did not have a happy ending. Saying how sorry she was wasn't going to help. Listening, however, might, so she bit her lower lip and made no comments.

"Most of the people who knew my parents were fooled, as I said. The counselors were new to the situation and Dad had changed after Mom left so they began to be suspicious."

If Colt's story had been in a book, Brooke might have skipped ahead to see what had happened. Her mouth was getting dry and her stomach was beginning to feel upset. He had stopped looking at her and was staring into space as they continued to walk along the sidewalk.

"The police searched our house and questioned me, of course. Dad made all kinds of excuses and I'd been at school so I was no help at all. Finally, they brought in a K-9 like Sampson. He found her."

Brooke covered her mouth to stifle her words. "Oh, no," she gasped.

"Yes. Dad had killed her and buried her in the yard. I watched them find her body from my room upstairs. Saw the whole thing."

"He went to prison?"

"Oh, yeah. And died there not too many years after. I stayed with Mom's parents until I was out of college. They were wonderful. Even took me to church, something my father had forbidden Mom to do."

"That must have helped," Brooke said, knowing by their past interactions that he shared her faith.

"It did. Eventually. I had to release a lot of bottled-up anger first, but I finally turned to Christ and realized what a strong presence He'd had in my life all along. I don't think I'd have made it if not for Jesus. I really don't."

Blinking away unshed tears, she asked, "Why are you telling me all this?"

Colt stopped, put down his go bag, turned to face her and grasped her shoulders. "To remind you that even somebody who seems normal may not be. Forgiving them may be the only way to find peace but that doesn't mean you should ever trust them."

"You were able to forgive your father?"

Tears tipped over her lower lashes and trickled down her cheeks when she saw Colt shake his head.

"That's how I know it's vital," he said. "I am making progress since he passed away in prison, though."

Instead of whisking away her tears, she stepped closer, slid her arms around his waist, laid her cheek on his chest and offered consolation the only way she knew how, with another embrace.

There they stood, in the middle of the day in a strange city, acting like long-lost friends or loves. Brooke knew she should be embarrassed and hoped her forwardness hadn't caused him to feel that way.

Confirmation that she'd done the right thing under the circumstances came when he slipped both arms around her and returned the hug.

It didn't last nearly as long as Brooke would have liked. When Colt released her and stepped back, so did she, taking pains to avoid looking at his face for fear he, too, was overly emotional. How hard it must have been for him to reveal that story. Nobody had to tell her he didn't do it often. That was evident.

Finally, when he picked up the small duffel that was his go bag and started to walk again, she joined him and said, "Thank you."

No reply came from Colt, nor was one expected. Brooke intrinsically knew how special his confession had been and how much it had cost him to make it. She also realized, for the first time, how well he was able to hide the injured part of his heart by joking and seeming to laugh at the minor inconveniences of life. His ready sense of humor was more than fun. It was medicine for his scars and balm for the unhealed wounds he still suffered.

SIXTEEN

Colt picked up the keys to the rental car and opened the trunk to stow their bags. He'd brought a laptop, too, and kept that up front even though he figured his smartphone would do anything he needed.

"You're on speaker," he told Donovan via his cell. "We're in the car and will be heading for the last known address of the Parkwell Adoption Agency first. Even though their landline is disconnected, someone here in Hungry Horse may know where they've gone."

"Affirmative. There have been several reports of Stevens's double since you left Washington, so we're pretty sure she didn't follow you, although one possible sighting was at the athletic field you took off from."

"Okay. Thanks. Feel free to catch her while we're gone. Don't wait for us."

"Good of you to offer to share the glory," his chief quipped. "Keep me posted."

"Will do." Ending the call, Colt propped the phone in the center console and glanced over at Brooke. "Ready?"

"Listen, if I could fly in that tiny helicopter without getting hysterical I'm ready for anything."

"You didn't act petrified," Colt told her as he pulled out into traffic.

Brooke chuckled. "Then I'm in the wrong profession. I should be acting in movies. Might even get an Oscar."

"That bad, huh?"

"Almost. We all pretend. Even levelheaded professional cops like you. It's how we survive the things we have no control over." She paused. "Like me finding out I might have a twin."

"You know you do."

"Yeah. Let me enjoy pretending I don't for a while longer, okay? I'm afraid I'll be faced with plenty more proof soon."

"That's what we want."

"Need, you mean. I'm pretty sure I don't want to confirm that my alter ego is running around killing people." Brooke hesitated, then said, "What I don't get is why she didn't clobber me when she had the chance."

"Beats me," Colt said, "but I'm happy she didn't."

With a wry chuckle, Brooke agreed. "You and me both, my friend. You and me both."

Instead of the commercial facility Brooke had expected, the former Parkwell Agency had been in a large, private home. The sign out front was faded and the paint was flaking but there was no doubt they were in the right place.

Brooke knocked on the front door. No one answered. She tried again while Colt shaded his eyes and tried to look in through the porch windows. The home was dark, almost forbidding, at least in Brooke's active imagination. It was hard to believe she had actually come from a place like this.

Unable to raise anyone by knocking, Colt went one way around to the back of the house and Brooke went the other. By the time she reached a vegetable garden in the back, he was speaking with a diminutive, gray-haired woman.

Colt waved and called to Brooke, "This is Lynn Park-well. She and her sister used to…"

As the elderly woman began to turn, Brooke watched her eyes widen and her jaw go slack. Then she shrieked and ducked behind Colt.

Brooke could tell he was as confused as she was by the intense reaction. She hurried up to Lynn and offered a greeting. "Hi. I'm Brooke Stevens."

There were tears and fear in the woman's eyes. She finally managed to speak but remained hidden behind Colt as if that would protect her. "You're—you're not Tina?"

"Is that her name? Tina?" Brooke asked.

"Yes. Tina Daniels."

"And we're twins?" To Brooke's relief, the woman seemed to be accepting her and relaxing.

"Yes. Tina is my sister Rita's daughter. I didn't know exactly what had happened during the births until Tina found Rita's diary. Oh, I suspected plenty, but poor Rita had wanted a baby all her life and I didn't have the heart to deny her. Not after she'd managed to breathe life into little Tina."

"Maybe we'd better sit down for the rest of your story," Brooke suggested. "I'm really confused."

Lynn nodded and led the way to a picnic set beneath an oak that was just starting to leaf out. She brushed off the seats with her hands, then gestured. "Please. Can I get you something to drink? Coffee? Tea?"

"No, thanks," Colt said. He took the woman's elbow and helped her into a chair. "Let's start at the beginning. You and your sister ran an adoption agency here?"

"Yes. We named it Parkwell, after my late husband, and arranged private adoptions. We had a doctor on staff for a while and Rita was trained as a nurse. She never married but she dearly wanted a child. While I was handling your adoption to Mr. and Mrs. Stevens, Rita and the doctor were looking after your birth mother. She was a transient and I'm sure she gave us a false name. All she wanted was to deliver her baby and see that it got a good home."

"What about my twin?"

"I'm getting to that," Lynn said. "The doctor wasn't satisfied with the birth. He wanted a sonogram but we didn't have that kind of sophisticated equipment so he was working blind. By the time he realized there was a twin, enough time had passed since your birth that the second baby was in serious distress. Tina was finally delivered but it had been too much for your birth mother and she didn't make it."

"Why didn't you offer the other baby to my parents?"

"They were already gone by the time Tina was stabilized. Rita didn't even tell me she was caring for a second little girl she'd resuscitated until several days later. She cried and cried, begging me to look the other way, and I'm ashamed to say, I did. I know it was breaking the law to falsify documents and lie about Tina, but I loved my sister. She'd literally saved that baby's life. How could I separate them?"

"Why did you act so afraid of me just now?" Brooke asked, trying to be understanding and squelch the ire she was feeling on behalf of her twin sister.

"Tina always had anger issues. Looking back, I can see it clearly. Rita loved her, of course, and spoiled her, too, so there is that. When we lost Rita a few months ago, Tina was sorting through her mother's possessions, found an old diary, read it and flew into a rage. Rita had confessed everything, right down to the fact she'd wished your birth mother would die so there would be no complications to her keeping the second baby. The doctor was in on it and falsified a birth certificate indicating that Rita was the one who had given birth to Tina so she could never be taken away."

Colt's voice was low and slightly gruff when he interrupted. "You should know this—we think Tina is in Washington State and suspect her of committing murders there."

Lynn's tears flowed and she pressed her fingertips to her lips. "I'm so, so sorry. I never meant it to come to this and I know my sister didn't, either. If only Tina hadn't found that diary."

Brooke leaned forward and patted Lynn's arm. "What happened then? Did she hurt you?"

"She tried. I locked myself in the bathroom while she wrecked the house and scattered old records all over the office. When I saw you just now I was afraid she'd come back for me."

"Old records? Is that how she learned my name and where I was living?"

"I think so." Lynn was weeping. "It must be. I never dreamed she'd try to find you. I suppose she used her computer. She was very good at that kind of thing. Rita always said she hoped Tina would get a job in an office, where she could use her talents."

"She didn't?" Colt asked.

"No. Never could hold a job, probably because of her terrible temper. Rita did her best to smooth things over for the girl, but Tina believed unfair things were always happening to ruin her life. In the end, I think she blamed Rita for all of it."

Brooke knew what she should ask, yet hesitated. Colt met her gaze and seemed to tune in on the thought. He was the one who posed the question. "How did your sister die?"

"What do you mean?"

"Was it natural causes?"

As Brooke watched, the elderly woman seemed to shrink

on her already spare frame. If the sequence of events was shifted a little, Tina could have read the diary while Rita was still alive and done the unthinkable. Perhaps she had. Given the killings that had taken place at Mount Rainier National Park, it was certainly possible. Tina was clearly guilty of other murders and if she was convicted of those, she'd spend the rest of her life behind bars.

Colt stood, urging Brooke to do the same. "Is there anyone you'd like us to call for you, Mrs. Parkwell?" he asked. "You really shouldn't be alone until your niece is in police custody."

"I have a friend I can stay with," Lynn said. "She looked after me for a while when I had a sort of nervous break-down."

"Little wonder you're upset," Brooke said, trying to be kind despite the situation. "You're not responsible for what your sister did all those years ago and you're not to blame for Tina's rampage, either."

"I just wish I'd done things differently back then," Lynn confessed. She took a tissue from her pocket and blew her nose, then asked Brooke, "Will you pray for your sister? Please? She's had a rough life. Rita and I weren't able to give her all the expensive things she wanted. We did our best. It just wasn't good enough."

"I'll try," Brooke said honestly. "I promise I'll try. I'm still trying to wrap my mind around what happened and what my twin has been doing."

"Are you positive it's Tina?" Lynn asked.

Brooke nodded sadly. "The DNA evidence says so. It's either her or me and I know I didn't harm anyone. Plus, Officer Maxwell was with me when some of the incidents occurred. If the DNA left on the victims hadn't matched mine, we'd never have suspected there was someone out there who was just like me."

"She isn't, you know."

Curious, Brooke stared. "Isn't what?"

"Isn't like you. Not a bit. If I hadn't jumped to conclusions the minute I saw you I'd have realized it sooner. You two may resemble each other the way identical twins do, but whatever makes you the people you are is different."

"You couldn't have said anything nicer to me if you'd tried." After giving Lynn a quick parting hug, she stepped away. It was a stretch to consider the woman her aunt, but she did feel an affinity for her. "Promise us you'll get out of this house and stay out until Tina is caught."

Colt passed Lynn his card. "You can reach me here. It's my unit's headquarters. If you give me a number where you can be reached I'll see that you're kept informed."

"Thank you. Both of you. I wish I'd been able to help more."

"We have a name and identification now," Colt said. "Did Tina happen to take her mother's credit cards?"

"Rita's and mine," Lynn said. "I reported it, but the credit-card company said I couldn't cancel my sister's cards for her. They insisted Rita had to do it." She grimaced. "I tried to tell them it was impossible for a dead person to contact them."

"So Tina can't be using your cards?"

"No. Whatever Tina buys on credit will be in my sister's name or her own."

"Okay," Colt said, raising his phone to report to Donovan. "Don't keep trying to cancel those cards. They're one of the best clues we have."

Brooke ushered Lynn toward the old house to give Colt privacy to speak freely to law enforcement. "Come on, Mrs. Parkwell. I'll help you pack. We can give you a lift to your friend's house."

"That's sweet of you to offer." Lynn sighed audibly. "I had my own car but that's gone, too."

"Tina stole it?"

Lynn nodded.

"Okay, give me a description and the license number. Do you have a pen and paper I can borrow?"

Trying to phone Colt to tell him and finding his line still busy, she ran back outside with the new information.

"We have a vehicle description!" Brooke shouted to him, waving a slip of yellow paper over her head.

"Terrific! I still have my chief on the line."

Reciting the new information, Colt waited patiently. Brooke also waited, less patiently. It didn't take long for Donovan to track down the missing car. It had been abandoned at the Kalispell airport a month ago. They were back to square one.

SEVENTEEN

By the time they had taken care of Lynn Parkwell, returned the rental car, boarded the helicopter again and touched down in Olympia, it was nearly dark. The helipad was next to the impressive two-story building that housed the Pacific Northwest K-9 Headquarters.

Escorting Brooke in past the keypad lock that guarded the doors after hours, Colt explained, "Chief Donovan Fanelli's office is on the ground floor." He gestured with a sweep of his arm. "These desks in the open area are for officers and support staff. The break room, separate locker rooms and showers are in the back."

"Impressive."

"Thanks."

"What's on the second floor?"

"Our evidence room, a conference room and storage."

"Where's Sampson?" It was touching to see her concern.

"The training center and kennels are next door. Our vet is nearby, too."

Hesitating, Brooke looked around the deserted room. "Will we be flying back tonight or waiting until morning?"

"If I can get us accommodations in the apartments connected to the training center, I'd like to put off leaving until I can be sure Sampson passed his physical. You don't mind, do you?"

"I guess…"

"There are separate quarters for men and women," he added quickly.

"Of course, there are."

Colt could tell by the twinkle in her eyes that she was making fun of him and, true to his nature, he felt himself beginning to blush again.

Brooke laughed. "I think you got a little sunburned today."

"Bad genetics," he said before thinking about how the comment could be interpreted.

She sobered. "Yeah, there's a lot of that going around."

"I didn't mean you, you know."

"You could have. It doesn't matter. We are what we are. Nothing can change that."

Problems about where to stay were solved when Veronica Eastwood, one of the four candidates vying for two open spots on the PNK9 team who was staying in the training-center apartments, invited Brooke to bunk with her because her current roommate, Brandie Weller, was away on a training assignment. Colt thanked her profusely. "I really appreciate this, Veronica." He looked to Brooke. "We both do."

"No sweat. I'm scheduled to train with Peyton Burns and the bloodhound pups tomorrow. It'll be good to have somebody to talk to tonight instead of just pacing the floor. I'm really nervous, especially after that embarrassing incident about misplacing my gun and badge right in front of Chief Fanelli." She pouted briefly. "I still think Parker Walsh hid them so he could go with you to question suspects instead of me."

"He said he didn't. Look, don't worry. You'll do fine tomorrow," Colt assured her. "I'd like to show the pups to

Brooke, anyway." He checked the time on his phone then looked at messages. "The chief wants to debrief me in his office at nine tomorrow morning. Suppose I come by here at eight, get Brooke, and we go claim Sampson together?"

"Fine with me." Brooke made a silly face. "I won't be late for work. I don't have a job to go to until we find our suspect." Her smile blossomed. "Besides, I love puppies."

Colt chuckled. "These are more like teenagers than tiny pups. If you think Sampson is fun to watch, these guys will have you in stitches."

"I hope so," Brooke said. "I could use a little comic relief."

"Couldn't we all." He had waited in the doorway when Brooke had entered the small suite. Now, he backed up so Veronica could close the door.

The hallway was fairly quiet except for the sound of a radio or a TV coming from one of the other rooms. Surprisingly, he hated to walk away. Yes, Brooke was perfectly safe. And, yes, she'd be comfortable. That wasn't his problem. So what was?

It didn't take a trained psychologist to tell Colt he'd formed an emotional attachment to the sweet-tempered ranger. The sense of their belonging together was growing stronger by the minute and it seemed the harder he fought against it, the closer he felt to her.

Forcing himself to walk away, Colt was determined to stop those destructive thoughts. He'd known since his teens that he was never going to marry, never going to take the chance there might be too much of his father in him, and the older he got, the more certain he was. Rather, he had been certain until he'd met and gotten to know Brooke Stevens.

Was it wise to rethink his decision? Not in his view. The more he cared about Brooke's well-being and future, the more he realized he shouldn't even consider becoming a part of it. She deserved better. Much better. Just as she didn't deserve to end up with a murderous sister, she didn't need a husband who might snap, the way his own father had.

Thinking back, he'd known his dad had a volatile temper but had never dreamed things would progress to the killing of his loving mother. The memory of losing her in his early teens was as vivid as when it had happened. So was the arrest of his father and the way the man had flailed and shouted and tried to beat off the police sent to take him into custody. That much violence was so frightening, Colt had been imprinted. The love of his mother and her parents did the same, of course, but those memories were tender and gentle, so they had had a lesser influence over the way he'd chosen to direct his adult life.

Never, in all the passing years, had he been tempted to revisit his decision to stay single…until he'd met Ranger Brooke Stevens.

Settled into the small quarters with her hostess, Brooke wasn't surprised to notice textbooks on crime and forensics. What also caught her attention was piles of research on cold cases.

"Looks like you love your subject," she told Veronica, pointing.

"That's a side interest of my roommate, Brandie Weller. We're both candidates for openings in the K-9 unit—us and two guys, Parker Walsh, the guy I mentioned, and Owen Hannington. Like Brandie always says, we can learn a lot from history and never know too much about what makes the bad guys tick."

"Yeah, tell me about it," Brooke said. "I just found out I have an evil twin."

"You're joking, right?"

"Nope. I wish."

"Sorry. That's such a cliché I thought you had to be teasing me." Closing her laptop and leaning back in her chair, Veronica ran her hands over her close-cropped, tight black curls and laced her fingers behind her head. "Want to tell me about it?"

"Sure. Why not?" Launching into the story from the time that crime-scene techs had found her DNA on the body behind her cabin and matched it to samples on the first hiker, and ending with the trip to Hungry Horse, Brooke tried to repeat details logically and in a workable order. When she was done, she said, "There. Since you're more into criminology than I am, what are your views?"

"Hmm. DNA is more my sister Jasmin's field of expertise. She's the unit's tech specialist."

"I thought your last name sounded familiar. Is she the reason you're trying to join this unit?"

"No. I would have applied even without her being involved. I'm just hoping nobody thinks I have an advantage because we're sisters."

Brooke huffed. "Having a sister can be a definite *disadvantage*, too."

"Yeah, no kidding. I was going to say you got a raw deal until you got to the part about your twin being essentially stolen and raised by a woman who was paranoid about losing her all the time she was growing up. What did you say her name was?"

"My twin? Tina Daniels. We don't know what she may be calling herself now, but if she's still using her late mother's credit cards we hope we can trace her that way."

"It's possible. The matching DNA was a giveaway. You had no idea? Not even a glimmer?"

"Nothing."

Brooke could tell her new friend was mulling over the clues, so she stayed silent to let her think.

"I'd always thought twins had some kind of bond. Guess not."

"It never occurred to me that I was somehow missing something. I'd always felt whole, complete, you know?" Brooke hesitated, wondering. "I suppose Tina might have sensed that something was wrong, but according to her aunt, she didn't tumble to our twin-ship until after her adoptive mother died."

"The diary. Yes, you mentioned it. There's no doubt that Tina is the guilty party?"

"None. DNA doesn't lie and we've actually seen her up around Mount Rainier. I forgot to tell you she forced Colt's SUV off the road and nearly killed us, too."

"I heard about that." The rookie smiled. "Everybody did."

"Yeah, I figured. It wasn't pretty but it wasn't his fault. Tina stole a delivery truck. It outweighed us."

Nodding, Veronica stared at nothing for a few seconds, then said, "What I don't get is her motive. At first it looked like she was trying to frame you and get you punished. Then she seemed to switch to direct attacks. That doesn't make sense."

"It didn't to us, either."

"You and Colt?"

"Yes." All of a sudden Brooke felt like a bug under a microscope. "He's trying to help me. It's all part of his job."

"Uh-huh. And the K-9 plays what part?"

"Sampson found the cadavers, just like he's trained to."

"And after that?"

"Well, he did some tracking and then he defended me. Twice. And got kicked for his trouble."

"No wonder the poor dog is here for a checkup. Was he acting hurt?"

"No, but Colt says big dogs are pretty stoic and he wanted to be sure Sampson was okay."

"That makes sense. Colt is ultimately responsible."

"I got him into trouble?"

The slightly younger woman grinned at Brooke. "Possibly, but judging by the look he gave you just before I shut the door, I don't think he minded one bit."

Bad dreams haunted Colt enough that he gave up trying to sleep and arose at dawn, threw on his uniform and headed for the kennels to check on Sampson.

One of the staff members was already on scene, hosing down the runs and getting the dogs ready for training. Feeding, he knew, would be done by the head trainer or each K-9's handler, if possible, to reinforce the training to not accept food from strangers.

The din of the dogs when he walked in was earsplitting. No wonder the man on duty was wearing earphones. Colt waved to get his attention, called, "Morning, Jonathan," then went straight to Sampson. There was a health checklist clipped to the run next to the dog's leash. His K-9 partner was in perfect shape. Relieved, Colt unclipped both, pocketed the note and opened the gate.

Sampson greeted him as if he'd been pining for him for eons and was finally rewarded with his presence. The canine's enthusiasm was contagious, bringing a grin and lifting Colt's spirits instantly.

He cupped the giant head and ruffled the dog's long, velvety ears. "I missed you, too, old boy." The ecstatic bloodhound slurped Colt's forearm, then lunged for his cheek so he straightened. "Down, Sampson. Settle."

Colt could tell how hard his canine partner was trying

to behave. Mostly successful, Sampson continued to wag his tail while looking up at his human with pleading brown eyes and happy panting.

"Good," Colt told him flatly to keep from feeding the excitement. "Heel. We'll take a walk and get you some breakfast before we go pick up your friend, Brooke."

At the sound of her name, the K-9 brightened, trotting a few paces before reining in his enthusiasm.

Colt laughed softly. "Yeah, I have to admit I kind of feel the same way. We'll keep that a secret, just between us, okay? No fair telling her that we like her."

It didn't strike Colt as at all odd to be confiding in a dog. It was, however, unlike him to entertain those kinds of tender human feelings, even unspoken. Oh, he liked female companionship and had dated plenty of nice women over the years, but the minute one of them started to take him too seriously or mentioned a shared future, he was history.

Was that the difference in Brooke Stevens? he wondered. Was her habit of pulling back and avoiding any hint of commitment what appealed to him? He supposed it could be. After all, she was embroiled in enough drama to last most people a lifetime so it was logical for her to avoid forming new relationships.

In that respect, he and Brooke were perfect for each other, at least on the surface, and now that she knew his family history he was positive she'd continue to shy away.

Memories of the hugs they'd shared contradicted his conclusions until he reminded himself of the extenuating circumstances. She'd been frightened and had needed comforting, that's all.

Except for the time when she'd offered her comfort to him, he added, recalling that event vividly. To his shame he'd let someone glimpse his pain, someone he barely knew. No more than three or four people were aware of his past and now there was one more.

That should have bothered him more than it did, he realized. His grandparents seldom mentioned his late father's terrible deeds and his boss, Donovan Fanelli, had never brought it up once.

Somehow, Colt knew Brooke would keep his secrets as well, even if he failed to ask her to. She was extraordinarily trustworthy and intelligent enough to sense the importance of his confession. To understand his need to keep it to herself, unlike many people, men and women, who loved to spread tales.

How sad that her own secrets, ones she hadn't even known existed, were about to become totally public. They had to be in order to find and stop her twin. Lives had been lost already and more were most likely in jeopardy, maybe even Brooke's.

Colt shuddered. Checked the time. It was too early to call for her, but he was going to head that way as soon as Sampson was fed.

Something inside him insisted he hurry. Maybe it was instinct, maybe imagination. All he knew was he had to be with Brooke, to see for himself that she was all right. And then make sure she stayed that way.

EIGHTEEN

Restless, Brooke had showered, dressed, made a pot of coffee and helped Veronica finish it by seven that morning. When there was a knock on the door, her heart almost jumped out of her chest. At least that was what it felt like.

Laughing on the inside, she hurried to answer, pausing with her hand on the knob as she called out, "What's the password?"

"Coffee," Colt announced.

"Drank it all. Try again."

Brooke could tell by his tone that he was amused. "Okay, donuts."

"That'll do." She yanked open the door and grinned up at him until she spotted Sampson and dropped to her knees to hug the K-9 the way a child would hug a plush teddy bear.

"Unhand my partner, madam," Colt quipped. "You're spoiling him rotten."

Truly penitent, she jumped to her feet and backed away, waving her hands between them as if to erase her errors. "I am so sorry. Veronica warned me, and I forgot already." She was eyeing the happy, drooling, panting dog. "He's just so adorable."

"Well, try to restrain yourself," Colt advised with a lopsided smile.

"I will. I am. I promise, I promise," she said, practically stuttering in her eagerness to make amends.

In the background, Veronica was laughing. That didn't help. Neither did Colt's quip. "If he had his working harness on I'd say it was the appeal of the unit patch and badge. I hear the ladies love a guy in uniform."

Brooke did chuckle lightly but doubted Colt heard her over the raucous laughter of her hostess. Well, so what if a man—or a K-9—did look handsome in a police uniform. So did park rangers. The shade of green or blue or khaki didn't matter nearly as much as the pride in a man's stance and the way his badge of authority lent credence to his formidable persona.

In other words, she thought, feeling her cheeks warming the way Colt's often did, the uniform gave him an aura of power, kind of like the Bible verse in II Timothy that said, "For God hath not given us the spirit of fear; but of power, and of love, and of a sound mind."

That wasn't a bad verse to quote, was it? Especially lately. The *power* wasn't nearly as necessary as the *sound mind*. And what about the love? Surely that referred to brotherly love, and that she had in abundance. There wasn't a thing wrong with admiring Colt Maxwell's dedication to his job and his K-9 as well as his cool head in an emergency. Given the choice of anybody else she knew, he was far and away the best person to have guarding her.

Not to mention that his dog is adorable, Brooke added, trying to stop her mind from going forward in the same vein. It was no use. She had to admit it. The K-9 cop was appealing, from his curly blond hair and blue eyes all the way to the toes of his polished boots.

Especially his tender heart, she added. Without that he'd be just a normal, nice guy. Instead, he was unique to the point of being extraordinary. That was a good thing in this instance. A very good thing. The problem was, she would rather not have noticed and it was far too late to keep from admiring him almost to the point of hero worship. Emotions aside, that was *not* acceptable.

Colt cleared his throat. "Ahem. If you're ready to go, grab your stuff. I'll give you time to visit the pups while I speak to the chief, then we'll leave for Mount Rainier."

Delighted for the distraction, Brooke thanked Veronica, scooped up her small bag and jacket and joined him at the door. "Ready."

"Looking forward to your chopper ride later?"

Brooke rolled her eyes. "No. I just want to get back to my park and catch a killer."

"Being focused and goal-oriented is good."

"So is success," Brooke said. "We're going to get her. I know we will. The alternative is unacceptable."

She walked with Colt down the hall, out the doorway at the end of the building and into the kennel area. A din of barking began before they arrived and continued even after they'd reached the run that contained the three puppies.

"Whoa. You weren't kidding," she said with a wide grin. The young bloodhounds were standing on their hind legs, making them nearly as tall as she was. "These are seriously big babies."

"Told you so. Meet Agent, Ranger and Chief. They were named by the grandson of the man who arranged the grant that funds my unit."

"Can I go in with them?"

"I'll have to get permission first." Colt had pulled out his phone and started to call the head trainer when he spotted her at the end of the walkway. "Hang on. Be right back."

Watching him approach a slim, attractive woman and shake hands with her, Brooke felt a stab of jealousy and proceeded to chastise herself. The only reason for such unsettling feelings would be having a personal interest in Colt, and she didn't. No, sirree. Not one bit. Not an iota. Not a… Oh, who was she kidding? She had it bad for the guy, and his opinion of her was probably the worst. After all, Tina was running wild and hurting people and they shared identical genes. Brooke figured she might as well have a big red circle with a slash through it tattooed on her forehead.

Before she had time to come up with further signs of her unsuitability, Colt came jogging back. "Twenty minutes," he said, opening the gate and blocking the enormous pups so Brooke could sidle in. "I'll check in with the chief, then come back for you. If you need any help, Peyton Burns, our head trainer, is right over there. Tell her if you need a break."

"What will their specialties be?" she asked as he started to turn. "Cadaver dogs like Sampson?"

"They'll start out in basic scent detection and then each will be trained in either narcotics or tracking—whether people or illegal weapons or cadavers," Colt said. "Peyton has been training them in Mount Rainier National Park through all sorts of terrain—from mountain cliffs to ditches to forest to crowded public areas—in all sorts of weather, at all times of day. In another few months, they'll be ready to be permanently paired with handlers."

"Lick!" Peyton called and the puppies each gave Brooke a kiss.

Brooke laughed as the rambunctious bloodhounds cavorted at her feet, stepping on her toes and bumping her legs so hard she had to lean against the fence to stay upright. Extending her hands to try to pet them, she found her fingers thoroughly licked by all three, and they weren't very good at taking turns.

"Hey, cool it, guys," she said, still laughing and enjoying the interaction. "Sit. Sit? Please, sit?"

To her surprise and delight, they obeyed. Not neatly and not quickly, but their rear ends did touch the ground. Sort of. The posture looked enough like a sit to satisfy her. "Good boys."

A quick glance at the trainer showed Brooke she had been watching. At least the woman wasn't scowling at her. That had to count for something. Normal pets like dogs and cats had not met with her mother's approval, so her parents had paid for Brooke to take fancy riding lessons and in the process of learning how to ride a gaited horse, she'd also had a chance to make friends with the barn cats and ranch dogs at the stables. They were what she had missed most when her parents had decided she needed a more refined hobby and had sadly switched her to dance classes.

The antics of the pups drew her out of the melancholy left over from childhood and reminded her that no matter how rough she'd once believed her life was, she'd had it easy compared to poor Tina.

Would she have turned out like her sibling if she'd been subjected to the same scrutiny and paranoia? Brooke didn't think so, but, truth to tell, she wasn't sure. Day-after-day pressure could be detrimental to the most levelheaded, easygoing person, child or adult.

Still, she reasoned sensibly, Tina had stepped over the line and could never go back. Even when terrible sins were forgiven by God, the consequences remained. Yes, it would help her twin to learn about the Jesus that Brooke followed, but belief and repentance weren't going to erase the past. Even the passage of years couldn't do that, as Colt had learned.

Compassion for him filled her. They had both been affected by the acts of others and were paying a bill they didn't owe.

No, it wasn't fair. It wasn't right. It simply *was*. Only the future could be changed and that depended, more than she liked, on past history, good or bad.

They were airborne again when Colt signaled to Brooke to listen to the report he was receiving. A woman matching her description had been found, injured and confused, on the same trail where Brooke had been attacked. The victim was being transported to the hospital in Ashford.

"It can't be that easy. Not after all the effort to find out who she was and where she came from."

Colt sympathized. "I know. It seems kind of unfair. Given all the trouble she's caused, you wanted to hunt her down yourself, right?"

A smile started to cross Brooke's face and she shrugged. "Well, maybe not exactly hunt her down, but close to it. I did want to face her again and speak to her instead of just standing there mute the way I did before."

"You still can. I can take you to the hospital to visit her."

"Do you think that would be allowed? I mean, she has to be under guard, right?"

"I certainly hope so. When I spoke with my chief this morning he told me they're in the process of checking her DNA, but he's one-hundred percent sure she's the killer we've all been looking for. He also confirmed she looks a lot like you."

"Ya think?"

He chuckled. "Yeah. Go figure. An identical twin who's identical. What a concept." Seeing Brooke start to get misty-eyed, he tried to distract her while still sticking to the subject. "I don't recall the exact statistics but, as I told you before, only about ten percent of twins who look alike are genetically identical. Differences occur when cells are dividing and fail to perfectly copy all six billion base pairs."

"Only six billion, huh?"

"Yeah, it's a tiny mutation at first and that may be all it ever is. When that cell goes on to form more of the body and the change is passed on, that's when the identical DNA is changed or damaged."

"Humph. It would be nice to think I didn't get the killer gene but since our DNA is close enough to the same for your CSIs to pick me as the murderer, I probably match in that way, too."

Colt reached back from the front seat of the chopper. He couldn't have touched her hand if she hadn't held it out to him. "Your fingers are cold."

"Forgot my gloves."

He said, "I'll get you mine," and tried to pull away.

She held tight. "No. I'm fine. I just…"

"Just what?"

"Just wish I didn't have a cold-blooded killer in my family."

Tugging harder, he freed his hand and turned back around to watch the country pass below the chopper. If he'd thought about it he'd have turned off the mic in his headset before he said, "Ditto."

Brooke stewed about her faux pas for the rest of the trip. She hadn't been thinking of the story Colt had told her about his parents because she'd been too focused on her own problems when she'd mentioned family. Of course, he shared her history. And he'd had a lot longer to suffer from it. Citing her personal feelings without specifying whom she'd meant was unforgivable.

A substitute silver PNK9 Unit SUV was waiting for them when they landed at Ashford and it only took ten minutes to reach the hospital. She'd expected Colt to be upset and continue to refuse to chat with her just as he had at the end of their flight. What she had *not* expected was the intense anxiety she began to experience when they entered the hospital together and approached Tina's room.

An armed Ashford police officer sat in a chair at the door, reading a paperback novel. Colt's uniform would have been enough to identify him but he showed his credentials as well.

"Have fun," the cop said. "She was wild when they brought her in so they gave her something. I don't think she'll be too talkative for a while." He eyed Brooke. "I can see a little resemblance."

She let the comment pass. A nurse was at Tina's bedside, checking her vital signs, when Brooke and Colt entered. One arm was strapped to a board with an IV dripping and the other was cuffed to the bedrail. Clearly, the patient was unaware of her surroundings but not totally unconscious.

Approaching the bed, Brooke felt tears welling. It was like seeing herself, worn out and ill-kept, with her hair tangled and scratches on her arms and face. "What happened to her?"

Colt checked his phone and found the preliminary report. "She was discovered on one of the trails in Rainier Park. It looked as if she'd been beaten and left there. Your fellow rangers thought she'd been the victim until a teenager with a cut on his head and a black eye showed up to report that he'd been berated then jumped by a demented ranger and had fought back until he could get away to run for his life."

"I still don't understand her motive for attacking—and killing—anyone."

"I don't know, either," Colt said. "But hopefully, we'll learn that when we can question her."

Brooke nodded. "Tina finally attacked somebody she couldn't get the better of." Brooke sighed sadly and reached to smooth loose auburn locks off her twin's forehead and reposition the single bobby pin that held them. She looked to Colt. "Do you think I could stay until she recovers more? I'd really like to talk to her."

"A lot depends on the prognosis," Colt answered. "Charts are all on computer these days so I can't tell. Shall I go find a nurse or doctor?"

"Will they tell you anything? I mean, I thought hospitals had to keep patient records confidential."

"Not in the case of criminals. If she's actually been arrested, the chief should already know. If not, maybe he has a good idea, anyway."

"Can they arrest somebody without reading them their rights?"

"You really are on her side, aren't you?"

"Not about what she did," Brooke insisted. "I just know she has to be severely mentally ill and needs somebody to look out for her best interests."

"She's killed two young men and attempted a third murder today. She tried to kill us. At least twice."

"Not necessarily." Brooke knew it was futile to try to defend her sister, yet she really did identify with Tina, perhaps for the first time. "She shot at the SUV, not at either of us."

"*After* she pushed us over a cliff."

"It was a steep slope, not a cliff."

Colt threw both hands in the air, startling Sampson. "Have it your way. Stay here. I'll go see what I can find out and then speak with the chief."

Nodding, Brooke was penitent about upsetting him but firm in her decision to stay with Tina. The invisible bond that both Colt and Veronica had suggested was beginning to manifest itself. It wasn't that Brooke actually identified with Tina, it was more as if they shared a presence of some kind. They were separate people, yet they weren't.

Brooke reached for her sister's limp hand and held it gently. The fingers felt cold. There were calluses on her palm and the nails were short and jagged, probably bitten off. Worse, as she stroked Tina's wrist she felt ridges, so she turned it over and saw scars. Whether she'd meant to take her own life or not, her twin had been desperate enough to cut herself. Multiple times, from the look of it.

"I'm so sorry, honey," Brooke said softly. "I wish I could go back in time and hug you when your life fell apart and make all the hurt go away. No one should have to face disappointment like that all alone." She sniffled. "Maybe, if I'd been there, the truth wouldn't have broken you."

To her surprise, Tina's fingers trembled, then closed around hers as if she, too, sensed the bond.

NINETEEN

Tina roused and seemed to recover more quickly than Brooke expected. When their eyes met they both began to shed silent tears.

"I'm so sorry," Brooke said gently. "I wish we'd known about each other sooner. Maybe things would have turned out differently."

"I know." Tina was struggling to sit up despite the IV and a handcuffed wrist so Brooke adjusted the bed pillows to help her. "Thanks."

"How are you feeling?" Brooke asked.

"Pretty good, considering. I probably look terrible, huh?"

Brooke gave her a smile, sniffled and dashed away her own tears. "Nothing a washcloth and comb won't fix."

"Would you help me? I think there's a comb in the bathroom."

"Of course. You'll feel better once your hair is smoothed down. I can't do much for the bruise on your cheek, though." She paused and considered her sister. "What were you thinking? I mean, why attack hikers? You killed two innocent young men. And why dress up like me? I never did anything to you."

Tina averted her gaze. "I don't know."

"Yes, you do. You must. Please?"

The misty eyes that looked up from the bruised face seemed sincere. "I—I guess I wanted to mess with your perfect life. They always said I was a troublemaker. Maybe I figured it was time for you to see what it was like to be me."

Brooke could have countered that she would never be like Tina, but chose to keep that to herself. The young woman had enough problems without being forced to face the gravity of her mistakes. Besides, the police wouldn't want anyone interfering in their plans to question Tina later.

"All right," Brooke said, making an effort to keep her voice even and her tone gentle. "I'll help you fix your hair."

"Can you wet the comb in the bathroom and bring me something to wash my face? I feel grimy." Tina asked plaintively.

"All right. Hang tight. I'll be right back."

A niggling little voice in the back of Brooke's mind warned her against trusting her look-alike while logic insisted that anyone who had been beaten, handcuffed, then drugged into a stupor, was no danger to anyone.

When she returned mere seconds later, however, the bed was empty and a partially straightened bobby pin lay atop the white sheets along with the abandoned IV needle and tubing.

Her breath caught. Everything went dim. She felt herself falling, then almost floating, and sensed pain…

Opening her eyes, she found herself lying in the hospital bed dressed as a patient. Her wrists had been tied to the bedrails with strips of gauze bandaging and there was adhesive tape covering her mouth.

A scream welled up, muffled by the tape, and echoed inside her aching head.

* * *

It hadn't taken Colt long to get permission to speak with an attending physician.

"We did an MRI and CAT scan on Daniels when she was brought in," the on-call doctor said. "There was no brain swelling."

"How long before she wakes up?"

"Ah, that. Paramedics gave her propofol. They had to dose her to get any cooperation. She needs rest so we haven't tried to reverse it."

"In other words, you don't know."

"Educated guess, four hours, give or take."

"And how long has she been sedated?"

The doctor circled the nurses' station and leaned over to access Tina's records again. "About that long. She should be stirring soon."

"Okay. Thanks."

Without waiting for a reply, Colt rushed to the elevator with Sampson still at his side. The ride up was interrupted by stops at two other floors and each time the patients or staff boarding took way too long to suit him.

From the end of the hallway, he could see that the local officer was still on duty and Colt's nerves began to settle some. Any altercation inside Tina's room would have disturbed the guard and he'd have gone to investigate. The fact that he was still relaxing outside the door was a good sign.

Colt slowed to a normal brisk walk. Sampson walked beside him, panting and wagging, obviously eager to rejoin Brooke. That amused Colt. "You're not as excited about it as I am," he said quietly.

Starting to nod a greeting, Colt was brought up short when the cop stood and stretched. "Your friend left. Said she'd be right back, though."

That wasn't right. Why would Brooke leave when her

purpose for staying was to talk to Tina? Had they quarreled? Were Brooke's feelings hurt? It was possible, he supposed, although if she'd decided to leave, surely she'd have notified him.

He laid a hand on the door, then began to push it open slowly, cautiously, to keep from agitating Tina. The auburn-haired patient in the bed was thrashing and obviously trying to shout past the tape over her mouth. In an instant his mind filled in the blanks and he shouted to the guard. "Get a doctor!"

Instead, the befuddled cop stuck his head into the room. "Why?"

Anger filled Colt. "Just do it." He crossed the room in three long strides. Tears were coursing down the sides of Brooke's face and wetting the hair above her ears. The tape came off with difficulty—it hurt him when he was forced to hurt her in order to help.

"I'm sorry, honey. I tried to be gentle." He cut both restraints and Brooke rubbed at where she'd been tied.

"She tricked me. I thought we were getting along fine and then…" She felt around in the bed, found the bent bobby pin and held it up. "She must have used this. I never dreamed it would work to unlock the handcuffs."

Colt groaned and shook his head.

Covering her face with her hands, Brooke wept more. "I was too gullible. I let my guard down. She's the most convincing liar I've ever met."

"Are *you* okay?" he asked. "Dumb question, I know."

Brooke threw both arms around his neck and held tight. With one arm supporting her shoulders, Colt wrapped a light blanket around her, slipped the other arm beneath her bent knees and lifted her into his embrace. She continued to cling as a nurse entered the room.

"You don't have permission to get this patient out of

bed," the RN said firmly. "Put her back immediately." Through the open door, she called for the reluctant guard. "Officer, I need you in here."

"You don't understand," Colt insisted. "This isn't your patient."

"Look, mister, I don't care how many badges you have or what your credentials say, this hospital has rules. Put the patient down."

"Is a doctor coming?" Colt asked.

Instead of answering, the nurse said, "I'm calling Security," and picked up the phone next to the bed.

"Good. Tell them there's a murderer loose in this hospital and to seal all the exits immediately," Colt ordered. Continuing to carry Brooke, he commanded Sampson to heel and pushed his way out of the room.

"Stop!"

A male nurse and the cop watching the door blocked Colt's way as if they intended to interfere. One warning bark from Sampson stopped them in their tracks.

Colt retraced his steps to the ER and took Brooke straight to the emergency-room doctor. "This isn't the same woman you know as your patient," he said firmly. "This is her twin, who Tina Daniels attacked before taking some of her clothes and fleeing. I think Brooke may have a head injury. She was groggy when I found her."

A puzzled expression didn't stop the medical man from reacting professionally. He gestured. "Bring her into this cubicle and put her on the gurney so I can take a look."

Although Brooke was conscious, she kept her arms around Colt's neck until he gently grasped her wrists and drew her arms down. Trained to recognize head trauma as part of his education, Colt nevertheless wanted the doctor's opinion before he was willing to relax control.

Standing to the side, the doctor said, "Turn her hands over and show me her wrists."

As Colt did so, the doctor physically blocked the arriving security guards. "No scars from self abuse. He's telling the truth. This isn't the same woman I admitted."

Colt was relieved but still angry. "You heard him. Lock this place down before your real killer gets away."

Logic had already convinced him that it was too late but he felt obligated to try, just the same. If Tina Daniels was half as wily as he thought, she was already out of the hospital and well on her way to causing more mayhem.

His main concern now was Brooke. If one more person died as a result of her being too trusting, too naive, she was bound to take it personally. She was already identifying with her twin. Going forward, her angst was going to keep building until they either recaptured Tina or somebody died.

His greatest fear was that Brooke's turbulent emotions couldn't handle whatever happened next. His fondest hope was that she could and would. He was certainly going to do all in his power to get her through.

Scenes of the short time spent with her sister kept flashing through Brooke's mind as she donned the set of blue hospital scrubs the nurse had provided. If anyone else had behaved the way she had and let Tina escape, she'd be the first to criticize. Granted, she hadn't realized her twin had something to pick the lock with. But what was wrong with her? She knew her twin's murderous history. Why in the world had she felt so sorry for her?

One thing was certain. She did *not* belong in law enforcement. In the past, the temptation had been to further her career by advancing beyond a level-one ranger. That was never going to happen. Not after this fiasco with her twin. If the park service took her back—big *if*—she planned to stay right where she'd been, happy and fulfilled by teaching novices about nature. That was assuming her ~~boss ever forgave her for getting involved in Tina's escape.~~

And not just her boss, Brooke mused. Most of the park rangers and K-9 cops were probably pretty upset with her, too. Truth to tell, only one of them mattered enough to cause her undue concern. With Colt so angry at the hospital security force and ready to personally throttle the cop who had let Tina pass so easily, it was hard to tell if his rancor extended to her. As soon as things settled down she planned to ask him.

A nurse had taken Brooke's blood pressure and pulse after she'd dressed. The doctor was holding his index finger in front of her face. "Follow my finger with your eyes. Don't move your head."

She did as he asked, blinking when he shined a bright light into her eyes, one at a time, then flashed it away.

"Good. Pupils equal and reactive." His fingers probed her scalp. "Any sore spots?"

Brooke planned to deny injury until he touched a place that made her jump and wince. "Ouch."

Colt immediately reacted. "Bad?"

"No, no. I was just surprised. I didn't think she'd done any damage."

"Can she go, Doc?" he asked. "I'm supposed to deliver her to Mount Rainier, and we're already running late."

"Ms. Stevens could stay with us for observation," the doctor said, "although I'm not detecting any lasting damage."

"Uh-uh." Colt was adamant. "I'm sticking to Brooke like glue. We're not going anywhere without her."

"By we, you mean you and your dog?"

Colt nodded, glancing at Sampson, who had made himself at home, crawling as far beneath the exam cot as he could get. "Yes."

"I really feel okay," Brooke offered. "I don't want to hang around here when there's work to do back at the park."

The physician scribbled something on a form, signed it and handed it to one of the nearby nurses. "You're done. Try to stay out of trouble," he said lightly.

Brooke understood that the doctor was merely making polite conversation, but judging by the glare Colt was giving him, not everyone in the cubicle was ready to exchange casual remarks.

She swung her legs over the side of the gurney and dropped the few inches to the floor. "Okay. Let's go back to Tina's room, get my boots—if Tina didn't steal those too—and hit the road."

If Colt had followed any closer he'd have been stepping on her heels, and that proximity was making her more nervous than she already was, which was actually quite a feat.

Holding up a hand, she stopped. "I'm okay. Steady and not a bit dizzy. You don't have to be ready to catch me. I'm not going to faint."

Despite backing off and resuming a more normal manner, Colt made a sour face. The expression was so fleeting she'd have missed it if she hadn't been looking right at him when it happened. Well, fine. Let him stay unhappy with her for a bit. It beat feeling as though he was about to pick her up and run with her like, he had after he'd freed her from Tina's bed.

She sighed as they made their way outside. Sun was peeking through a smattering of clouds and the rest of the day promised to be more like spring than what they'd been having. Maybe park visitors would even get to see the mountain instead of fog or low clouds. That would be grand.

"Where are we going first?" she asked as they climbed into the SUV with Sampson.

"Ranger headquarters. Henning's office. Donovan caught a chopper as soon as I told him Tina got away from us. He'll meet us there."

"Got away from me, you mean."

"No. From us. I should never have left you alone with her."

"There was a cop at the door, she was handcuffed and barely conscious when you left," Brooke countered. "You didn't do a thing wrong. I was the one she tricked."

"Were you?" He pulled into traffic and headed east on Highway 706. "Has it occurred to you that she could have been faking her semiconscious state all along?"

"Not until just now it didn't." Brooke's brow furrowed and her eyes narrowed. "That would fit with the kind of person Lynn said Tina was. Devious."

"Yes, it would. I think…"

When Colt didn't finish his sentence, Brooke scowled at him. "What? What do you think? Tell me."

"Never mind. It was a dumb idea."

"Let me be the judge of that, will you," she said. "I'm the expert on dumb ideas."

Watching him, she could see the struggle between his desire to tell her and fear of doing so. Finally, he said, "The best way to fight her and win may be to play by her rules."

"I hope you don't mean I should become a big a liar."

"No, no. Nothing like that. I was thinking of trying to trick the trickster. Laying a trap for her the way she did for those unfortunate hikers and who knows who else."

"Me."

"Yeah, you, too, although you escaped in far better shape than they did, with the exception of the one who fought back this last time."

"Tell me what you have in mind."

Colt shook his head vigorously. "Not yet. Let me run it by Donovan first and see what he says. Georgia Henning will probably have to be in on it, too, and probably a few officers and dogs from my unit."

Brooke began to smile at him in spite of his sober expression. "Let me guess. I'm the bait in this trap of yours, right?"

"I wish there was a better way, but I can't come up with one."

"I love your plan," Brooke said. "Anything that will atone for my mistakes works for me."

"Even if it's dangerous?"

She chuckled softly. "Being related to Tina Daniels and not knowing where she is puts me in a lot more danger than you're talking about. Tell your chief I'm in."

If Colt hadn't turned to her with such intense concern brimming in his blue eyes she would have added "all the way up to my neck," and laughed at the imagined danger. Here was a man whose go-to mood was to tease and she was seeing him nearly in tears. That was enough to touch her deeply and leave behind a blossoming sense of being loved that she hadn't expected.

What took her aback even more, she realized, was her readiness to return whatever affection he offered and not question anyone's motives. That was almost scarier to Brooke than the idea of facing her murderous missing twin.

TWENTY

Colt took Brooke with him to his meeting with Donovan as soon as she'd changed clothes. Sampson joined them in Henning's private office.

The chief was seated at the head ranger's desk and wasted no time with pleasantries. "Sit down. Both of you." He checked the screen on his phone. "Since Tina's hospitalization and escape, no more hikers have reported being attacked."

"Ending up as the victim for once may have wised her up," Colt told his boss.

"More likely she realized she couldn't pin anything on Brooke anymore. Either way, we can't let down our guard. The first thing I want you to do is take Sampson hunting for bodies, just in case."

"What about Brooke? I don't want to leave her. Tina's crafty."

"And some people are easier to fool," Donovan said with a telling glance at Brooke.

Colt was about to stick up for her when she spoke in her own defense. "I don't know why she was able to convince me she was trustworthy. I knew better than to turn my back on her then and I know better now. I've been trying to rationalize it ever since she overpowered me and tied me down."

"Maybe being her twin affected you," Colt suggested.

Brooke nodded. "I've thought of that. It did feel strange when I looked at her and saw myself. I can't imagine actually identifying with somebody like her, but I suppose it's possible. I can't think of any other reason for my risky behavior."

The chief steepled his fingers in front of his face. "She is family."

"No, no, no. I didn't let her escape on purpose if that's what you're suggesting. The only conclusion I can come to is that my heart must have overruled my brain. Trust me. It was a temporary condition. It won't happen again."

"Time will tell."

"Yes," Brooke said, "and Colt has a plan that will prove whose side I'm on. We believe Tina will come after me if she's given the chance and I've agreed to act as bait."

The chief snorted and shook his head. "You have this all figured out, huh? What makes you think anybody else will agree to some off-the-wall plan that puts you in danger?"

"I'm responsible for Tina's escape," Brooke said with conviction. "Everybody knows that. Whether they place total blame on me or not, I had a big piece of the action. I should be allowed to volunteer my services to atone for my mistakes."

"Not if it costs you your life," Donovan said. "We know she's a killer."

"I'd be right there with her," Colt replied. "And we can bring in as many others as you see fit." Pausing, he studied his boss's face and guessed he was close to agreement so he went on. "Brooke needs this, Donovan. She knows she made an error and is more than ready to put things right. Give her that chance? Please?"

Chief Fanelli pushed back his chair and laced his fingers together on the desktop. "My first instinct is to forbid it but I do see your point. I won't promise anything now but I will discuss a possible plan with Georgia Henning and a few of my people." He stood. "In the meantime, I want you covering the remote areas Daniels is known to have used before. If there are other victims, I want them found, not only for the sake of their families but because they may provide further clues. Considering all Tina Daniels has done I have to wonder if she's been working alone."

Stepping forward, Colt inserted himself between Brooke and his chief. "You can't seriously think Brooke is involved."

"I never said that," Donovan countered. "But as wily as her twin is, it's possible she's convinced somebody local to help her."

That, Colt could accept. "Okay. My mistake. Sorry."

"Apology accepted." He leaned down to check a file on his computer and print out a page, which he handed to Colt. "These are reported disappearances."

Colt scanned the list and frowned. "Wait a minute. These are from months ago."

"Right. I went back and started counting anything that took place after the death of Rita Daniels since you discovered that that event triggered Tina's first rampages."

"Are we positive she didn't have anything to do with shooting Stacey Stark and Jonas Digby?" Colt asked.

Donovan handed him a page of forensics findings. "Ninety-nine percent positive. If she did, she used a gun that was only accessible to law enforcement and left behind none of her DNA, unlike the killings we know she committed with Stevens's gun."

"Tina admitted she was doing that in the hopes of framing me," Brooke said. "I agree with Colt that she'd see the futility of continuing but I suppose she might have started before we realized it. She doesn't seem like a person who makes a lot of mistakes, though."

"I agree," the chief said. "Which brings us back to your plan for Brooke to lure her in. Why would she fall for that? She's had more than one chance to harm her and didn't."

With a sigh, Brooke said, "That was when she felt she had other options to get even. Those are gone. If she wants vengeance on me for living a better life, her only choice now is a personal attack."

The chief arched an eyebrow at Colt. "You're sure about this?"

"As sure as anyone can be. Even if Tina only comes to Brooke to talk, we can nab her."

"All right. Come up with a solid plan. In the meantime, I'll speak with Henning and get her onboard."

Colt was tempted to roll his eyes and might have if they hadn't been using the head ranger's office. "I take it I have your permission to take Brooke with me while Sampson works the trails."

"Until I tell you differently. I'll send Danica Hayes and Hutch with you for backup." The chief stood and began to smile slightly as he eyed Sampson seated at Colt's feet. "Your K-9 may wish he was an attack dog but he's no Hutch."

"Only because he wasn't born a German shepherd," Colt countered, relaxing enough to return the smile without having to force it. "It's his mama and daddy's fault." The moment the words were out of his mouth he realized how they may have affected Brooke and his grin disappeared.

Apparently in tune with his thoughts, she said, "It's okay. You don't have to keep avoiding the subject of heredity. It's the elephant in the room and far too big to ignore so we may as well acknowledge it."

"I am sorry," Colt told her.

"Don't be. There's nothing I can do to alter my past. I know that. What I have to do now is figure out how to live with it. I'm still trying to come to terms with having a twin, let alone a dangerous one."

"I think you're doing a great job, considering," Colt said. Looking to his chief, he expected at least a nod of agreement.

Instead, Donovan picked up the phone on the desk, pushed one button and spoke. "We're through here for now, ma'am. You can have your office back. I will need to speak with you at length later today, though."

The reply on the other end of the line must have been positive because Donovan nodded. "Tell your people to avoid the trails that Stevens usually covered. I'm closing them down and sending a team out to investigate today. I'll let you know when you can resume the nature walks."

Brooke tapped Colt's shoulder and spoke aside. "Tourists and hikers need one of those trails to access the Long-mire suspension bridge."

"Affirmative. We'll start there first and work our way back."

"You're familiar with it?"

"Oh, yeah," Colt said. "When you've seen murder victims and been shot at you tend to form strong memories."

"Stark and Digby, right?"

"Yes. As the saying goes, I hope it isn't déjà vu all over again."

Brooke was glad to have Danica's company on patrol but her real gratitude went to Hutch. The formidable black-and-tan German shepherd looked alert and ready to conquer a world full of criminals all by himself. Sampson, on the other hand, continued to remind her of a teddy bear. He wasn't soft and cuddly, of course. Under all that loose skin he was solid muscle, but his soulful eyes and long ears gave him a less aggressive look.

The forest near the path to the bridge was as beautiful as ever. Peaceful. Serene except for a couple of squirrels squabbling and running up and down Douglas firs on tiny feet that looked as though they barely touched the bark.

Brooke smiled when she noticed Sampson's momentary lapse of concentration on the trail ahead. "I think there was a hunting dog in your pal's family tree. Looks like he's noticing the wildlife."

"As long as he keeps doing his job, I don't mind. One of these days when I have time off maybe I'll remove his working gear and let him run around for fun. He knows the difference."

"I get it," Brooke said. "When I'm out of uniform it feels strange to be walking around out here."

"Surely, you hike when you're not on duty."

"I do. But I dress for it. I should at least have a radio and my backpack with a canteen." She let her gaze drift to the treetops, sensed a moment of dizziness when wispy clouds moved across the open blue and held out her arms for balance. "Whew."

"You okay?"

"Fine." Brooke laughed. "I always get a little disoriented when I look straight up and see the tips of the trees enclosing a little circle of sky."

"Um, then don't look up?"

She laughed. "How did you get so smart?"

"My grandma says I got it from Mom."

"Are they still living? Your grandparents?"

"Thankfully, yes, although their age is showing. Come to think of it, so is mine." Pantomiming an aching back, he took a couple of limping steps.

Brooke made a sound that mimicked a startled buck.

Colt grinned. "Did you just snort?"

"Merely demonstrating my nature calls," she said. "That was a deer. You should hear my angry-bear imitation."

"Save that one for your twin," Colt quipped. "If anybody deserves it, she does."

Falling into step behind Colt, with Sampson in the lead and Danica and Hutch at the back of the line, Brooke thought of Tina. She was too clever to be easily fooled. Too wary to fall for a simple ruse. Whatever they decided to do, it would have to be elaborate and executed with precision.

"So what are we going to do about her?" Brooke asked. "Tie me to a post and cover me with honey?" Behind her, Danica chuckled, encouraging her to keep teasing. "No, wait, that's for luring rogue bears. Probably shouldn't do that."

Seeing Colt roll his eyes gave her the giggles. She tried to suppress them, but it was no use.

"A little keyed up, are we?" Danica remarked.

Brooke had to agree, which set off her laughing again. The K-9 cop was right. Her nerves were stretched so tight she was suspended between hysterical laughter and hysterical screams, the key being the hysterical part. Maybe she and her twin weren't that different after all.

Momentarily absorbed by that premise, Brooke quickly pushed it aside. She and Tina were as different as night and day, both of which could hide danger, but Brooke saw herself as the sunshine, the one who delighted in making others happy and keeping the peace. And Tina? She was more than darkness, at least now she was. Tina was the personification of death, whether she realized it or not. Was it too late to reach her? Was she beyond help, beyond redemption?

Brooke believed that no one was ever too far gone to be forgiven by God. But that wasn't all there was to it. Tina needed to realize how wrong she'd been and let go of the anger that was tearing her apart, then ask for forgiveness in order for it to be granted. Reaching into her twin's heart and making that point strongly enough that Tina believed it was not going to be simple, if it was even possible. And then there were the consequences that didn't just disappear.

Brooke sighed, her good humor gone. A sermon of inspiring words was not going to sway someone so bent on revenge. Perhaps nothing would, but she had to make the effort.

First, however, they needed to find her wayward sister and keep her from doing more damage, lethal or otherwise. Right now that was the most important part of their task. Later, when things settled down and the threat was under control, perhaps she and Tina could sit down and have a calm, sensible talk.

Assuming we both survive, Brooke added, realizing she wanted that more than anything. It wasn't enough to merely get through this dilemma herself. She wanted to save Tina, too. Nobody had been there to speak for the second twin when she'd needed it as a baby. It was high time someone offered to help. Somehow.

TWENTY-ONE

When Sampson stopped moving back and forth, then put his nose to the ground and took off through the ferns and lush undergrowth that lined the trails where the sun reached the ground, Colt knew why. Presumably, his companions did, too, since he heard Brooke draw in a ragged breath.

He signaled to Danica. "Stay back with her, just in case." He didn't have to check to be sure his fellow PNK9 officer would. They'd trained for situations like this. Someone always stood guard while the others pursued their quarry. Sampson was doing exactly what he'd been trained for. He'd either sensed another cadaver or was on the trail of Tina Daniels, hopefully the latter.

Topping a rise, he spotted a campsite in an unauthorized area. Someone had been burning green-colored clothing and wisps of smoke curled upward from the ash. Chances were good that Tina, or someone aiding her, was disposing of clues that would tie her to the previous murders. He radioed his find, rewarded Sampson with the bunny toy and waited for rangers and the CSI team to arrive. Sampson had taken him too far off the beaten path for him to still see Brooke and Danica, but with Hutch on duty, he wasn't worried. Much.

Staying back to keep from contaminating the ground around the fire, Colt satisfied his concern by radioing Danica.

"I heard" was the first thing she said. "Fresh, do you think?"

"Definitely," Colt replied. "I managed to pull a partially burned ranger jacket out of the remains and it looks like there's blood on it."

"Tied to the Daniels murders?" Danica asked.

"Not necessarily but probably. I don't want to guess."

"Right. Well, you should know that Hutch is half-asleep from boredom and I'm not far behind him. We spent the last two days looking for lost kids and we're both bushed. Any reason for us to stay out here?"

"Somebody has to protect Brooke."

"I thought you'd taken on that job," Danica teased.

"Then you can protect me while I look after her," Colt countered. "Pull up a stump and make yourself comfortable until the cavalry arrives. That's what Sampson and I are doing."

"Fine, fine. In case you were wondering, our ranger is about to wear a rut in this trail from all her pacing. You'd think she was uptight or something."

"Yeah, or something." Colt knew he should not even consider leaving the crime scene unguarded, yet he desperately wanted to be close to Brooke. He took out his cell phone, checked it, then resorted to the radio again. "I have no cell service out here. How about you?"

Danica answered. "Nope. Not even a glimmer of a bar. Mountains are in the way, I guess. It happens."

"Right."

Colt retreated farther into the undergrowth, convincing himself he was looking for a suitable place to rest and wait. Truth to tell, he was also hoping to reach high enough ground to be able to see the portion of the trail where he'd left his companions, as well as keep an eye on the campsite. Once he'd admitted that ulterior motive, he stopped and leaned against the trunk of an enormous tree.

Sampson made himself comfy at Colt's feet and chewed on his stuffed pink bunny. The forest warmed in the rising sun. Birds called to each other, and small animals skittered through the underbrush, making the fresh green shoots tremble without wind. A long, deep breath of the pine-scented air reminded Colt why he loved these assignments that got him out of town and into the pristine landscapes of all three Washington State national parks, primarily Mount. Rainier, but also North Cascades and Olympic when Sampson was needed. He'd also never been more conflicted about his future than he was at present.

Colt let his mind explore the unexpected thoughts he'd been having of late, thoughts of turning his back on his past and embracing a brighter future he could now envision for the first time in his adult life. Was it possible he'd make a good husband and father some day? That concept was new, and yet it seemed almost plausible. Oh, he still remembered where he'd come from and what his father had done in a fit of rage, but maybe he hadn't inherited those tendencies. Or, maybe, his faith in God and decision to follow Jesus had saved him in more ways than one.

Lying on a pile of leaves at his feet, Sampson had switched from happily chewing the stuffed toy to licking it with his broad pink tongue. Suddenly, Colt saw him freeze, lift his head and stare off into the thick forest.

Birds fell silent. Not a single blade of grass moved. A brittle twig snapped as if stepped on.

Colt straightened and undid the safety strap on his holster, all the while listening for any break in the heavy silence.

Slowly, purposefully, Sampson stood, the toy forgotten.

Peering back at the camp scene, Colt saw nothing wrong, nothing different. Besides, that wasn't the direction Sampson was looking.

Colt reached for his radio and keyed the mic. "Danica? Are you hearing or seeing anything odd?"

"No, but Hutch is acting like he does. What about you?"

"It's too quiet," Colt said softly. On full alert, he took one step, then another, checking his surroundings carefully. He raised the radio again, intending to report activity near the fire, when he heard a dog begin barking.

That was followed in milliseconds by the sound of a woman's scream.

At Danica's side, braced for battle, Hutch set up a racket that echoed up and down the canyons before fading away in the vast wilderness.

Brooke stretched out both arms to block the K-9 cop and her dog. "Hold him still and don't make any sudden moves. If that's a sow with cubs and she's just come out of hibernation, she'll be cross."

"Did you ever see a sweet bear?" the other woman whispered.

"They mostly avoid people. The only reason she'd attack is if she felt her babies were threatened." In total ranger mode, Brooke said, "Keep the dog quiet. If she comes after him, let go of the leash and let him fend for himself."

"No way. We're partners."

"He's better equipped to run or fight than we are." She was still whispering. "See the way she's swaying? She's not sure about us."

"I'm not real sure about her, either," the PNK9 officer said softly.

Without warning, the mother bear jerked her head to

one side, gave a loud huff and plunged into the densest vegetation, disappearing in seconds.

Before Brooke had a chance to say a word, Colt and Sampson burst out of the trees onto the hiking trail. Hutch barked. Sampson barked. Colt demanded, "What happened?"

"A bear," Brooke and Danica said simultaneously.

Colt muttered, "A bear," as if he was still taking it in, then bent over with his hands resting on his knees.

Relieved beyond belief, Brooke smiled. "Yup. We're pretty sure Tina sent it to eat us. You know how ornery she can be."

"Not funny."

His bad mood didn't deter Brooke. "Oh, come on. We should be celebrating. It's spring and that bear was probably a lot unhappier to run into us than we were to see her. Besides, she lives here. We're the interlopers."

"Yeah, yeah. Well, since we're all together again why don't you two come with me. I'd like to see if Brooke recognizes the burned jacket."

"Will your backup be able to find us?" she asked.

Danica piped up. "They'll have the satellite coordinates. They should be able to walk right to us."

That suited Brooke a lot better than being separated from Colt, although she wasn't about to admit it. As soon as he straightened, turned and headed back through the trampled undergrowth, she was right behind him with Danica and Hutch following.

"It's right through here," he said, pointing as Sampson again took the lead.

They stepped into a small clearing. Colt threw out his arm to block the others. "Stop!"

"What's wrong?"

"The evidence I saved from the fire. It's gone."

Danica drew her gun. So did Colt. They stood with their backs to Brooke, aiming out.

Colt spoke. "You're the nature expert. Do you think the bear might have taken it?"

"I doubt it. We have more trouble with them stealing provisions from camps or getting into the garbage bins." She started to pass her protectors. "There should be tracks. Let me have a look."

"We go together," Colt ordered. He nodded to Danica.

"Don't even think of shooting my bear," Brooke warned. "I mean it. If you see her again you'd better not be the aggressor."

Going forward cautiously, she scanned the turf, paying special attention to the matted grasses in the area Colt had indicated. Adult bears left tracks as large as the span of her hand and their footprints would be impossible to miss.

The first signs she saw were shoeprints. Brooke halted. Pointed. "Look."

"Boots."

"Yes," Brooke said. "One set is the same size as mine. The other must be Colt's because I see Sampson's with them. The predator we're hunting is far more dangerous than a hungry bear. She's human."

She watched as Colt and Danica skirted the prints and approached the woods. The dogs were both eager to plunge in, but their handlers held them in check.

The last thing Brooke wanted was to see her protectors leaving her to follow whoever had made those tracks. She knew it was Tina. It had to be. The only question remaining was, had she been alone? And how had she gotten back to Mt. Rainier so fast after escaping the hospital in Ashford if she hadn't had help?

Apparently Colt was asking himself the same things because he bent to examine the ground and called Danica over. "I only see signs of one extra person. What about you?"

"Just the one," the K-9 cop answered.

"I doubt she went far after the beating she took," Colt said. "Stay here while Sampson and I trail her."

Inside, Brooke was screaming at him—*Don't go, don't leave me.* On the outside, she remained calm.

At least she thought she was until Colt looked straight into her eyes and said, "Don't worry. I won't let you out of my sight again."

"What if the…? I mean, what if she…? Oh, never mind. Just go."

Danica stepped closer. "It'll be all right. We'll stay right here."

Although Brooke wanted to argue, she kept it to herself. The logical K-9 to track was Sampson and if Tina was working alone, as the clues suggested, she couldn't have gone far. That conclusion would have been comforting if she wasn't worried about what her twin might have in mind for Colt. Or for poor Sampson, truth be told. They both mattered to her. A lot.

"If you tagged along he'd have to concentrate too much on *you*," Danica said. "His mind and all his senses have to stay focused on the job or he's in trouble before he starts."

"Thanks," Brooke said with a nervous chuckle. "I didn't know my idea to follow him showed."

Although Danica was still alert, still standing ready for defense with Hutch providing the keen senses humans lacked, she laughed softly, too. "I might not have been so quick to pick up the romantic vibes if I hadn't fallen in love with Luke Stark last month."

Brooke's jaw dropped. "Who said anything about *love*?"

"Apparently neither of you, but that doesn't make it any less true."

"We're chasing my homicidal sister. Why would anybody want to fall in love with me?"

"Beats me. I was never going to have a family, yet I fell for a guy with a baby boy. Luke is a little marriage-shy because he jumped into it the first time, but he's buying a house in Eatonville and going to work as an EMT. When and if we do decide to get married, we'll have the perfect place to live." She grinned. "Go figure, right?"

"It's not inevitable. Colt has the choice to reject me the same as I have the choice to stay single," Brooke countered.

"Doesn't look to me as though either of you have written off the other. Don't be too quick to decide. Give it time. You haven't known each other long."

Brooke sighed. "We haven't even dated."

"Not unless you count all the hours you've been thrown together. How many dates would it take to add up to that much time?"

Brooke had to smile. "I thought you were going to say 'quality time.'"

"Whatever. It's all subjective."

"It's mostly confusing," Brooke countered with a lopsided smile. She was about to explain why she thought so when they heard a call from the woods.

"Found it!"

TWENTY-TWO

"She didn't go far before she tried to bury the remains of the jacket in a pile of leaves," Colt reported to headquarters via radio. He hadn't moved the telling clue, but he had managed to place himself within sight of Brooke and Danica until other rangers and CSIs had arrived to take over.

Danica had been ordered to put Hutch on the trail of the person who had moved the burned jacket. Colt was glad to return to ranger headquarters with Brooke and Sampson.

"It might not be necessary to set a trap for Tina," Brooke said. "Hutch may track her down today and this will all be over."

Although Colt nodded in agreement, he was far from sure. Their K-9s were exceptional, but they couldn't track a person who escaped in a car or boat or whatever. Tina, assuming it was her, had set them up again and might have been successful in drawing him away and attacking Brooke this time if the chief hadn't sent Danica along as backup.

As they waited in the break room at ranger headquarters, he speculated to Brooke in the hope that getting her input would focus his ideas. "I'm confused. It seems to me, if Tina had wanted to harm you physically, she'd have done more when you encountered her in the hospital."

"I've thought of that."

As light hit Brooke's face, he couldn't help but notice how attractive her freckles were with her sun-burnished auburn hair and long lashes. "And?"

"And, it seems to me she did enough damage when she hit me." Brooke gently rubbed the back of her head.

"Tell that to all the others she's hurt. You got off easy compared to them."

"True. If it hadn't been for you believing in me and looking for reasons for matching DNA, I could be in jail, awaiting trial for murder, thanks to her."

"Somebody would have tumbled before that happened," he reassured her. "Probably your parents' high-priced lawyer."

"Lawyers, plural." She smiled slightly. "They would have earned their fees if they'd had to defend me on my own." Her gaze met Colt's and he couldn't look away. "Thanks. For everything."

He chose to make light of it by feigning a Southern accent, tipping an imaginary hat as he said, "My pleasure, ma'am." To be honest, it *was* a pleasure to be around Brooke, one that kept taking him by surprise in spite of prior experience. Colt figured that was probably because each time he considered his feelings for her, they were stronger. At this rate he'd be proposing marriage before they even had a chance to get to know each other. That incongruous thought made him smile.

Brooke noticed. "What's so funny?"

"Me."

"Oh, I don't know. That wasn't a very good imitation of a cowboy hero."

"Where did you get the idea I was trying to be a cowboy?"

"Maybe because every now and then you sound Texan."

"I do not." Colt was grinning. "You're baiting me, aren't

you? Why don't you just ask? My grandparents live in Oklahoma. They're the ones who introduced me to working dogs. They had heelers to help handle a few cattle." He sobered. "When I first went to live with them, those dogs were my best friends. My only friends."

"Looks like nothing has changed much," Brooke said.

"You're probably right. I've always related better to canines than to most people. Dogs are loyal and honest and they never gossip."

"You don't think they do. Maybe every K-9 in your unit knows everything personal about all you cops. They just don't let on."

That had him laughing. "In that case, I'd better stop telling Sampson all my secrets, huh?"

"You have secrets?"

Colt gave a nonchalant shrug. "A few. I already told you my worst one." And the only ones that really counted now pertained to his fondness for a certain park ranger with auburn hair and freckles and the prettiest hazel eyes he'd ever seen.

"Tell me more."

Colt knew she was teasing. When he said, "Not in a million years," however, his reply sounded more serious than he'd intended and he realized Brooke had picked up the difference.

"I'm sure you have plenty of secrets, yourself," he said, trying to smooth things over.

"Other than a lethal twin, an illegal adoption in the family, DNA to die for and a father who thinks money will buy him the world, no."

"That's it? That's the best you can do?"

"For the present," she said, blushing even more. "When all this is over I may have a few more things to say to you."

Sorry he'd let prior opportunities pass when he could have spoken up, Colt decided to be as honest as he thought he dared. "We will need to talk, I think. No, I know we will. But not yet."

"No," she replied. "Not until Tina is in prison and I've seen a professional regarding my possible emotional instability."

"There's not a thing wrong with you, Brooke. You're not your sister."

When she looked deeply into his eyes and said, "You're not your father, either," Colt was speechless.

A plan to trap Tina was being discussed when word came that Hutch had lost her trail. Disappointed, Brooke was not thrilled with the overly simple plan and she said so. Chief Fanelli took the criticism well. Georgia Henning did not. Irate and making her opinion plain, she threw down a file folder and stormed out, slamming her office door.

"I knew she disliked me, but I had no idea she wouldn't be willing to set me adrift in a canoe with no paddle," Brooke said. Seeing the puzzled looks from Colt and Donovan, she pulled a face. "I was being facetious, although being *up the creek with no paddle* would probably work as well as your ideas to send me back to my cabin when everybody knows I've been suspended."

"You have a better idea?" Colt asked. He'd folded his hands in front of him on the table and was leaning forward. "I'm all ears."

"Tina is bound to be suspicious. I would be and I don't have her devious mind."

"Then what?" It was Fanelli.

"Beats me. I'd been expecting you pros to think up something stupendous. Sticking me back into my cabin is pretty lame."

"Not if we make a big deal of it." Colt looked to Donovan. "We were thinking we could stage a noisy argument, maybe by the visitor center or at one of the Stark Lodges.

Maybe both places. One of us can stick up for you while the other one insists Henning fire you. If we gather a crowd, all the better."

"A public fight. That's all?"

"What we want to do is create interest. Get people talking. That way, even if Tina isn't in the general area when we stage the scene, she's still liable to hear about it. The permanent residents of national parks are a pretty close-knit group. They'll spread the word."

"That could take weeks. We can't sit around waiting for Tina to decide the coast is clear and finally make a move."

"We know," Fanelli said. "That was where your boss was supposed to come in. We wanted her to put a time limit on it, say less than a week, so Tina would be forced to act quickly."

Brooke arched an eyebrow. "And?"

"*And* she refused, so we'll do it without her."

"I have a better idea," Brooke said. "How about putting me under house arrest for letting Tina escape? That way, if she does spot somebody with me, she won't be suspicious and you can easily say I'm being taken into Ashford for arraignment ASAP. I'll be a lot harder for her to reach or blame once I'm stuck in jail."

"I like the way you think, ranger Stevens," the chief said. "We'll do this your way. Colt? Do you agree?"

His nod was less convincing than Brooke would have liked but at least he didn't argue against her plan.

"Do you think you can act the part?" the chief asked her.

"If you mean nervous, antsy, depressed and slightly weird, I'm your actress. That pretty much comes naturally to me lately."

"All right," Donovan said. "Can you start tonight?"

As the formerly beautiful day gave way to evening, a pall fell over the park that signaled impending storms.

That could be either good or bad, depending on whether or not it deterred Tina.

Colt and Sampson were inside the cabin with Brooke and an armed ranger, Trent Willoughby. At the last minute, Georgia Henning apparently had a change of heart and showed up, too. Colt and the ranger greeted her knock with drawn guns.

"At ease, men." Georgia barked out the order as if she had jurisdiction over both of the officers. She went directly to one of the windows and peered out. "Surveillance in place?"

Willoughby replied. "Affirmative."

Colt knew Danica Hayes and Hutch were out there somewhere, too. Hutch knew Tina's scent as well as Sampson did and was the ideal choice for sentinel duty. Willow Bates and Star were backing her up with several of the rookies, ready to move in if needed. As far as Colt was concerned, the only glitch in their plan so far was the unexpected arrival of the head ranger. This operation only needed one boss and that was Chief Fanelli.

Catching Brooke's eye, Colt motioned her aside. As she joined him, she was slowly shaking her head. "If I'd known this was going to turn into a big party I'd have ordered pizza."

"Yeah, I know what you mean."

"There's no way my twin is going to show up when I have a cabin full of company."

"Agreed."

"And?"

"Give me a minute. I'm thinking," Colt said. If he was Tina, he'd try to cause some kind of diversion, something that would draw everyone away. He figured they could sit there and wait for her to act or he could do it for her. Either way, it might mean leaving Brooke alone. That, he was loathe to do.

He did, however, decide to pose the idea to his chief. Stepping aside, he turned his back on the group and made the call.

"Yes, I saw Henning go in," Donovan said. "Undoubtedly everybody did."

"Including Tina Daniels."

"If she's around, yes."

"We need to see Henning leave. And the ranger she assigned to be in here with us."

"Agreed." Donovan paused. "What about you?"

That was the question Colt didn't want to answer. Nevertheless, he did. "I can wait outside with the rest of you, I guess. I just hate to do it."

"I hate to give the order but sometimes sacrifices are necessary."

Suddenly, Colt's duty was crystal-clear. "No. You can fire me for insubordination if you have to. I'm not leaving Brooke."

"Are you listening to yourself, Maxwell?"

"Yes, for the first time I'm hearing it loud and clear." Out of the corner of his eye, he noticed that she'd stepped closer. Her hazel eyes were misty, and she was gazing at him with evident fondness. He put out his free hand and she took it in both of hers as if the touch was a precious gift. Sighing, Colt ended his call with "Do what you have to."

He pocketed the phone and drew Brooke into his arms. "About that talk we were going to have…"

Lifting her head and looking up at him, she put one finger over his lips, then slowly raised in tiptoe to kiss him.

Colt felt as if iron shackles around his heart had been shattered, freeing him to love this extraordinary woman. As he held her, he noticed their pulse beats matched and their breathing was in sync.

She laid her cheek on his chest, her arms tightening around him, and made a soft sound that reminded Colt of a kitten's purr.

His mind said, *I love you, Brooke*, and he took a ragged breath to tell her so. Just as he opened his mouth, the piercing wail of a siren cut through the mountain air.

Brooke jumped away, her eyes wide, her lips slightly parted, and looked to him. "What was that?"

"Chief Fanelli," Colt said flatly. "His timing stinks."

Henning grabbed her radio and insisted on information. So did the other ranger. When Colt saw them peering at him, he answered his cell phone, fully expecting Donovan to tell him what he was doing.

Instead, when the chief did call, he said, "That's not me."

A rush to the door ensued with Colt and Sampson bringing up the rear. Once the rangers were outside, he stood back and watched them disperse to join members of the surveillance team.

By this time it was easy to tell where the noise was coming from. One of the park-ranger vehicles was in full pursuit mode, lights flashing, siren blaring. Its engine revved. Tires spun and threw rooster tails of mud. It was moving, faster and faster.

Colt put out his arm to block Brooke's exit as the heavy green, white and yellow vehicle sped into the yard.

He saw Henning dive out of the way at the last second and Willow Bates leap or fall backward, making it impossible to tell if they'd been hit or not.

The park SUV crashed into the woodpile with enough force to knock the bumper sideways, crumple a fender and break the windows. A white airbag deployed. An arm began slashing at it with a knife.

Pandemonium reigned as rangers and K-9 officers aided

the ones who were down and their dogs barked or howled repeated warnings.

Colt whirled and pushed Brooke in through the door, realizing that his K-9 was working. Sampson was locked on Tina's scent. Apparently Hutch was, too, because Colt could see the flash of brown-and-black fur followed by Danica's green uniform rapidly emerging from cover in the woods.

He looked back. The driver's door of the wrecked SUV was hanging open, the seat empty.

"Sampson, come," he called. Then, he saw him. Tina was running toward the cabin with the bloodhound tight on her heels. Brooke was inside. Colt and his K-9 partner were outside.

He faced the knife-wielding attacker, ready to draw and fire, when Brooke grabbed his arm from behind. "No! Don't shoot her."

Colt turned away for a mere second and yelled, "Shut the door." That was too long.

Tina shouldered into him and slipped inside with Brooke. Sampson slammed past Colt's legs and followed.

Out of options, Colt followed them in.

TWENTY-THREE

Brooke kept backing up until she ran out of space. The expression on Tina's face would have stopped her, anyway, if the wall hadn't. Intense emotion coupled with triumph glowed on her twin's face and malice glinted in her eyes.

Seeing the knife, Brooke grabbed a sofa pillow and held it in front of her. "Easy, please. I know you're upset, and you have a perfect right to be, but at least give me a chance to explain."

"There's nothing to explain," Tina yelled. "You got everything, and I got nothing. It's not fair."

"You're right, it's not," Brooke agreed. She purposely spoke more softly so her sister would have to quiet down to hear her. It was a tactic she'd learned from her mother, and it never failed to quell her dad's verbal tantrums.

Brooke held Colt at bay with the raising of one hand, palm out, and let Tina vent before she told her, "My mom and dad have said they would have taken you in a heartbeat if they'd known there were two of us."

"Yeah, right."

"They would have. You read about it in the diary, didn't you?"

"About your parents? No."

"Not them. About how you were born later and how the

doctor and the nurse, Rita Daniels, had to work to save you and our mother."

"She died."

"Yes, but you lived. ~~Think about it. Rita fought for you.~~ She breathed life into you when you couldn't do it for yourself." Brooke realized that could be an exaggeration, but it could also be true so she pressed on. "It's no wonder she fell in love with you and wanted to keep you so badly."

"I was her possession, not her daughter. She owned me. I should know. She told me often enough."

"Funny," Brooke said, meeting her twin's gaze and praying for wisdom. "I always felt the opposite, like I'd been given away because I was unwanted."

"They gave you everything. I know. I looked you up online. I saw the pictures of the house and the pool and the horses and the bracelet they gave you on your birthday." She displayed her left wrist. "It looks better on me than it ever did on you."

"I figured you'd taken it. Please, keep it as a gift."

"You think you can buy me?"

Shrugging, Brooke sighed. "That's what I thought my parents were trying to do when they gave it to me. I know they meant well but sometimes even the people who love us the most make mistakes."

"Love is a myth."

Despite concentrating on Tina, Brooke's eyes darted to Colt for an instant before she said, "No it isn't. It's very real," and lowered the hand that had been holding him back.

Tina was fast. Colt was faster. And Sampson proved the ideal distraction at just the right moment. He lunged for Tina's ankle while Colt grabbed the wrist of the hand wielding the knife. It was over in a millisecond.

He had possession of the weapon and had tightened handcuffs on Brooke's twin, then he said, "Put down the pillow and go to the door but don't stand there and give anybody a chance to make a mistake and shoot you. Open the door and stay back until they've seen me and my prisoner."

Still, Brooke didn't move. Colt saw the tears of compassion in her eyes and understood. She was grieving for what might have been with her twin just as he used to grieve for his lost mother. That kind of pain wasn't ever totally gone despite the popular notion of closure. Trauma left behind didn't disappear, it changed, softened, became part of a person's history and yet was also carried into the present and the future by unforgettable memories. Trying to put those out of mind was impossible, but learning to deal with them, to go on in spite of them, brought a kind of healing that was hard to explain.

And faith was what made it all work, he added to himself. Without faith in God and His Son, Jesus, life could seem hopeless, as it once had to him. Colt had come to the conclusion that turning to God for redemption wasn't the same as ceding control, it was trusting in a higher power and relying on divine love in even the worst situations. Once he had taken that step, he couldn't imagine how nonbelievers coped.

Colt holstered his weapon, marched his prisoner to the door, opened it slightly and called, "Scene is secure. Daniels is in custody."

Rangers and K-9 officers converged on the cabin. Colt turned Tina over to Danica, then went back to Brooke and gathered her in a comforting embrace. "It's okay, honey. It's over. For good."

"So sad," Brooke whispered. "Such a waste."

"But not one you could have prevented," he said wisely.

"No, I suppose not."

As they stood together and he gently rubbed her back, he could feel her relaxing. "It's too soon for our talk, I suppose."

Brooke smiled up at him with unshed tears gleaming. Raising both arms, she threaded her fingers through the blond curls at the back of his head and pulled his face closer. "It's not too soon for this."

Colt had no doubt she intended to kiss him again and nothing could have pleased him more. He bent to meet her lips and softly claimed what he had yearned for and denied wanting ever since they'd met.

Donovan's voice echoed from the open door. "Longmire Visitor Center in ten, if you two think you'll be ready to come up for air by then."

A giggle interrupted the kiss and Colt smiled. "The guy has a way with words." He sighed deeply. "I could stand here and kiss you forever."

"We can't," Brooke countered, grinning up at him.

"Why not?"

"Because we'd starve to death. I never did get around to ordering that pizza for my family reunion."

To Brooke's relief, nobody had been badly injured by her twin's rampage with the National Park Service SUV. A couple of officers had been treated for cuts and scrapes at the scene and Willow Bates had been driven by ambulance to Ashford. Word had come that she wasn't seriously injured but Brooke wanted to see for herself so she asked Colt to take her.

They were in the elevator on the way to Willow's room when Brooke said, "My folks have promised to have their attorneys represent Tina."

"She's currently under a seventy-two-hour psychiatric hold," Colt reminded her.

"If she's judged fit for trial, I mean."

"That's really extraordinary."

"They're great people. You're going to love meeting them in person. Mom says Dad has really come around."

"I am? You're inviting me?"

"Of course, I am." The elevator stopped and the doors opened, interrupting their conversation.

Seeing Willow preparing to leave her room, Brooke was delighted. "I'm so glad you're okay. We were all worried."

"I'm fine." The brown-haired K-9 officer's expression didn't live up to her statement.

"What's wrong?"

"Nothing," Willow insisted, picking up the plastic bag of her personal belongings.

Frowning, Brooke studied her. "Are you really feeling all right. You look a little green."

"Yeah, maybe."

"Nausea can be caused by a concussion," Brooke warned. "Did they check you out well?"

"Too well." Willow began to sniffle.

Brooke gently touched Willow's arm. "I'm a good listener. And I know how to keep a secret."

Although the other ranger did glance at Colt, her concentration stayed with Brooke. "Yeah? Well, it's more of a joke. And it's on me."

Waiting, Brooke leaned closer.

After several long minutes of silence, Willow caught a sob and said, "The test. The one they did because I was nauseated?"

"Uh-huh."

"It showed I'm pregnant."

"Whoa! Congratulations," Brooke said, meaning it and not understanding why Willow seemed so distraught.

"They'll let you keep working for a while, won't they?" She looked to Colt. "Won't they?"

All he did was shrug.

"Tell me what's really wrong?" Brooke urged the weeping K-9 officer. "Let me help you. Please."

"I don't know what to do. My husband, Theo, works for the FBI and…"

"Is the problem poor planning? I mean, not every baby arrives when it's expected. I'm sure he'll understand if you explain."

"No, he won't. We've been separated for almost three months."

Colt didn't say much until he and Brooke were back in the SUV and headed for Mount Rainier to see Henning about her reinstatement, since the crimes were now solved. He sensed her nervousness about her job and empathy for Willow's dilemma but wasn't sure if that was enough reason to put off telling her how he felt.

"Marriage is tricky, isn't it?" he began.

Brooke nodded, but averted her gaze. "It's people who keep secrets who're the biggest problem. Look at both our families."

That brought a wry chuckle. "I'd rather not."

Swiveling in her seat, she turned misty eyes on him. "We have to. You realize that, don't you? We have to decide if we're going to let the mistakes of others ruin it for us." She reached out for his forearm and gripped it, tightly but gently. "I don't want to do that. There's been enough hurt, enough lies, enough wrong decisions to last us ten lifetimes."

"Whoa. You're serious, aren't you?"

She didn't have to tell him where she was coming from. He knew because the thoughts she'd voiced were echoes of his own. After pulling to the curb, he parked, released his seat belt and turned to her fully. When she shied away a little, Colt reached for her hands and clasped them both. "Let's start with the easy part. I love you, Brooke."

Her jaw gaped. "What about Tina?"

"What about her? She's not you any more than my father is me. You just said it better than I ever could. We can't let the mistakes made in the past keep us from loving each other." He paused, his voice almost breaking. "You do love me, don't you?"

"More than anything. And believe me, I fought it."

Colt grinned. "You and me both, sweetheart. That's one battle I'm glad we both lost."

Brooke eased her hands loose long enough to unsnap her seat belt, then leaned into Colt's embrace. "Me, too."

"So what are we going to do about it?"

"Um, you could kiss me."

"Excellent idea." Cupping her freckled cheeks in both hands, he did exactly that. They were both breathless when he paused, then asked, "Anything else?"

Smiling at him, she blushed. "You could ask me to marry you."

"I thought I just did."

"Not exactly."

"I can't get down on one knee and offer you an engagement ring because I don't have one."

"I thought you K-9 cops were prepared for anything."

Colt had to laugh. Life with this woman was going to be one grin after another, with just enough mayhem in between from his job to make life unpredictable. Which reminded him of another concern. "Seriously, Brooke, you don't mind being married to a cop, do you? I mean, my job can be dangerous sometimes."

She laughed and slid her arms around his neck. "I face

down angry bears and territorial moose and snakes in the summer, not to mention tourists who think I can turn the rain on and off just for them and get mad when I tell them I can't. I think we're pretty equal in the danger department."

Colt was shaking his head, truly concerned that her teasing might be masking a deeper worry. "I said, *seriously*, lady. I mean it. Will my job bother you?"

"Only if you forget to bring Sampson home with you so I can hug him."

"What about me? I need hugs, too."

She blinked rapidly and a few tears trickled down her cheeks but she was still smiling. "So do I."

Relieved and filled with joy at the thought of spending the rest of his life with this amazing woman, Colt pulled her into his arms and held her, praying that his love and devotion would never fail, never disappoint her, and thanking God for bringing her into his life.

Then, he kissed her again.

* * * * *

Don't miss Willow's story, Explosive Trail, *and the rest of the Pacific Northwest K-9 Unit series:*

Dear Reader,

Once again I have been blessed to work on a K-9 series with fabulous writers. It's definitely a challenge since we are all working at the same time, but also satisfying when everything comes together. Actually, it's a lot like life itself, as various challenges meet us face-to-face. We wonder how we're going to make it, yet we do, and on the other side we can look back and see things more clearly. I, for one, know God has been with me and has brought me through lots of troubles in spite of myself. Help was always there. All I had to do was ask for it.

Thank you for following our series. It's our pleasure to present it to you.

Blessings,
Valerie Hansen

Get 4 FREE REWARDS!

We'll send you 2 FREE Books plus 2 FREE Mystery Gifts.

FREE Value Over **$20**

Both the **Love Inspired®** and **Love Inspired® Suspense** series feature compelling novels filled with inspirational romance, faith, forgiveness and hope.

YES! Please send me 2 FREE novels from the Love Inspired or Love Inspired Suspense series and my 2 FREE gifts (gifts are worth about $10 retail). After receiving them, if I don't wish to receive any more books, I can return the shipping statement marked "cancel." If I don't cancel, I will receive 6 brand-new Love Inspired Larger-Print books or Love Inspired Suspense Larger-Print books every month and be billed just $6.49 each in the U.S. or $6.74 each in Canada. That is a savings of at least 16% off the cover price. It's quite a bargain! Shipping and handling is just 50¢ per book in the U.S. and $1.25 per book in Canada.* I understand that accepting the 2 free books and gifts places me under no obligation to buy anything. I can always return a shipment and cancel at any time by calling the number below. The free books and gifts are mine to keep no matter what I decide.

Choose one: ☐ **Love Inspired Larger-Print** (122/322 IDN GRHK) ☐ **Love Inspired Suspense Larger-Print** (107/307 IDN GRHK)

Name (please print)

Address _____ Apt. #

City _____ State/Province _____ Zip/Postal Code

Email: Please check this box ☐ if you would like to receive newsletters and promotional emails from Harlequin Enterprises ULC and its affiliates. You can unsubscribe anytime.

Mail to the **Harlequin Reader Service:**
IN U.S.A.: P.O. Box 1341, Buffalo, NY 14240-8531
IN CANADA: P.O. Box 603, Fort Erie, Ontario L2A 5X3

Want to try 2 free books from another series! Call 1-800-873-8635 or visit www.ReaderService.com.

*Terms and prices subject to change without notice. Prices do not include sales taxes, which will be charged (if applicable) based on your state or country of residence. Canadian residents will be charged applicable taxes. Offer not valid in Quebec. This offer is limited to one order per household. Books received may not be as shown. Not valid for current subscribers to the Love Inspired or Love Inspired Suspense series. All orders subject to approval. Credit or debit balances in a customer's account(s) may be offset by any other outstanding balance owed by or to the customer. Please allow 4 to 6 weeks for delivery. Offer available while quantities last.

Your Privacy—Your information is being collected by Harlequin Enterprises ULC, operating as Harlequin Reader Service. For a complete summary of the information we collect, how we use this information and to whom it is disclosed, please visit our privacy notice located at corporate.harlequin.com/privacy-notice. From time to time we may also exchange your personal information with reputable third parties. If you wish to opt out of this sharing of your personal information, please visit readerservice.com/consumerschoice or call 1-800-873-8635. **Notice to California Residents**—Under California law, you have specific rights to control and access your data. For more information on these rights and how to exercise them, visit corporate.harlequin.com/california-privacy.

LIRLIS22R3

HARLEQUIN
PLUS

Try the best multimedia subscription service for romance readers like you!

Read, Watch and Play.

Experience the easiest way to get the romance content you crave.

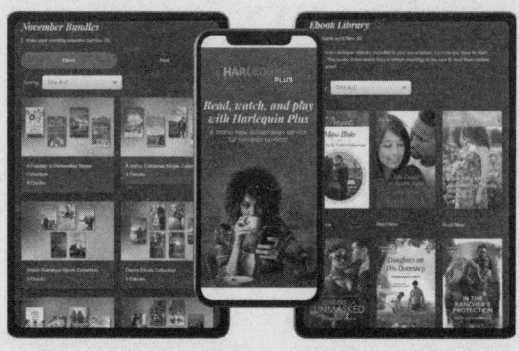

Start your **FREE TRIAL** at
<u>www.harlequinplus.com/freetrial</u>.